LINKED

Just what was Gregor Shenkov doing on his own in her old family home in Scotland? Victoria Mitchell had to wait to find out the answer—and to discover the link that tied them. . . .

LINKED FROM THE PAST

BY

MARY WIBBERLEY

MILLS & BOON LIMITED
15–16 BROOK'S MEWS
LONDON W1A 1DR

*First published in Great Britain 1984
by Mills & Boon Limited*

© Mary Wibberley 1984

*Australian copyright 1984
Philippine copyright 1984*

ISBN 0 263 74900 2

*Set in Monophoto Times 11 on 11 pt.
05–1084 – 52134*

*Made and printed in Great Britain by
Richard Clay (The Chaucer Press) Ltd,
Bungay, Suffolk*

CHAPTER ONE

It was dusk when Victoria arrived at Drummell House, the perfect time on a November day; slightly misty, the sky heavy with snow clouds. She loved Scotland in winter. She loved Scotland at any time, but winter was the best, with the memories it brought of huge log fires crackling, and walks in the snow. In a way, returning to Uncle Craig's had always felt like coming home.

The taxi driver slowed and turned his head slightly, interrupting her nostalgic introspection. 'How much longer does this drive go on?' he asked, puzzled. Victoria laughed. The way in to Drummell House, along three miles of densely packed trees at either side of the narrow driveway, always caused doubt in a stranger. No doubt he wondered if there *was* a house at the end of it. Victoria knew.

'Nearly there now,' she answered. 'See——' she leaned forward to peer through the windscreen as the dark turreted pile loomed, a black shadow out of the gloom.

'I see,' he said, and sounded doubtful, causing her to smile. Seen now, it had a grey ghostly sheen. 'Eh—you're expected then?'

Well might he ask. No lights shone at any of the many windows; all was silent. But then, he didn't know Uncle Craig either. He wasn't the normal idea of a host waiting impatiently in the hall for the guest to arrive, a welcoming drink at the ready.

He would most likely have his nose buried in a book, and not the faintest idea of the time, or even the day. 'Oh yes, I'm expected,' she answered.

The driver came to a halt in front of the imposing entrance. The house would have been better named Drummell Castle, thought Victoria as she stepped out and fumbled in her bag. She watched him remove her three cases from the boot, and then stand, looking upward, face expressionless. She wondered what thoughts were going through his mind, and could guess.

'Here you are, thank you,' she said, handing him the money they had agreed on when she had arrived at Aberdeen station. He had more than twenty miles' return journey. She had only a few more steps to take for the end of hers. He thanked her, lifted the cases, and deposited them at the top of the stone steps. She turned the handle of the front door, and it swung slowly open.

'Want me to wait a minute, Miss?' enquired the driver, putting the money and substantial tip she had given him into his back pocket.

'No thanks.' She moved towards the door. The hall was in darkness, but the glow of a dying log fire shone out, and she could feel the warmth from where she was standing. It was good to be there. 'Goodbye.'

'Goodbye now. You have my card if you need me.' The driver was backing away, still unsure, still puzzled, she could tell.

'Yes, I do. Thanks.' She watched him return to his car, a tall red-headed man who had told her his life story on the hour-long journey. Victoria had that effect on people, but she had never understood why. She never pried, never needed to ask questions, but people on trains, planes or boats invariably gravitated towards her, and told her their innermost secrets within five minutes of meeting her. A candid friend had once told her it was because she had the serene face of a madonna, and why hadn't she become a psychiatrist and made a fortune? and she had laughed about that, as she did about a lot of the nonsense her friends spoke, and treated it as no more than a joke. He waved from the car, then turned it slowly round, ready to drive home, and she waved back, then picked up the largest case, carried it into the hall, and put it down.

'Uncle Craig?' she called, and the words seemed to echo round her and fall into silence. She reached for the light switch and immediately the hall sprang into life and colour. The dying fire with ashes scattered in the hearth, the pile of logs near it ready to replenish it. She went over, bent and put two smaller ones on and the fire coughed and sparked and Victoria stood up, dusted her hands down and returned to the steps for her other two cases. She closed the door behind her and walked across the hall into the wide corridor leading to the drawing room. A touch of the switch and all was light. But there was still no answering cry from anywhere. Her footsteps were silent on the thick red carpet. The prints and old maps on the wall reflected the light. She knew them all by heart. She knew the smell of the house, that indefinable mixture of heather and peat, and smokey fires, and she loved everything there. She called again, but softly, as she entered the drawing room, and a small reading lamp was lit by the fire, and papers and books lay scattered in no particular order on the table by it, but of her uncle there was no sign at all. She walked over and studied the books on the table, and frowned. They weren't in English. They weren't even in the English alphabet, and that was stranger still. They were in what looked like Russian in the Cyrillic alphabet, and Uncle Craig had never mentioned that he spoke that, although he had a fair smattering of pretty well everything else.

She was about to turn, to go and look upstairs when a slight sound came from the doorway and she whirled round. 'Uncle——' the words she had been about to say died on her lips. A man stood outlined in the doorway, the light behind him silhouetting him sharply and for a moment she had the illusion that she was seeing an old portrait step into life from the past, for there was something other-worldly about him. Then, as he walked forward, the illusion was shattered, and she caught her breath in a strange sick sense of recognition—equally quickly banished as she realised that she had never seen *this* man before in her life.

He spoke. He had a deep voice, as deep as brown velvet, deceptively soft, and a strong foreign, instantly recognisable accent. 'Who are you?' he asked. Victoria took a deep breath, still shocked and surprised by seeing someone so different from her uncle. 'Victoria Mitchell,' she answered, equilibrium returning. 'And who are *you*?'

'My name is Gregor Shenkov,' the man answered. No possible doubt about the accent this time, and, as he walked forward, no possible doubt about the face, the high Slavic cheekbones, deep intense eyes under thick black brows, wide mouth that held no smile of welcome, or anything else. And he was a very big man. He was tall and powerful looking, broadshouldered and narrow hipped, wearing faded blue corduroy jeans and darker blue fisherman's jersey. She wondered, seeing him thus attired, how she could possibly have taken him for a medieval man. Yet there was something timeless about his appearance, some haunting quality, an unusual blend that made her pulses race. He looked—dangerous, some adventurer from another world, as indeed from his name and accent he seemed to be.

'I came here expecting to see my Uncle Craig,' Victoria responded. 'Where is he?' She saw brief surprise—or was it shock?—on his face, as if he did not believe her, as if he might indeed ask: 'Are you sure?' But he didn't. He said instead words that were to shock her:

'He is in hospital.'

'Hospital?' She echoed the word, her heart constricting in sudden fear. 'Why? How——'

'There is no need for alarm, Miss—Mitchell.' He hesitated over that last word as if he did not quite believe it, but Victoria was too stunned to note the subtle nuance. 'He is not seriously ill, but he has concussion.'

'I must go to him.' She was already moving towards the phone as she answered. There was a taxi firm in the village of Drummell five miles away. As she picked up the receiver she turned towards the man. He was watching her. He hadn't once taken his eyes off her since he had walked in. He had a dark intent gaze, as if he might be looking deep inside her, and that was disturbing too, as disturbing as he was. She wondered if she was going to faint. She had never fainted in her life, but the room seemed to shift and move and she put her other hand on the table to steady herself and fought to control the images that surfaced. She was apparently alone, here in this large house miles away from anywhere with a man who had reminded her briefly—but all too vividly—of another, Englishman, whom she loathed: this one a foreigner—no, more, a *Russian*—a tall powerful Russian who had *his* papers, *his* books scattered round as if he belonged there and intended to remain for some time, and he had just told her that Uncle Craig was in hospital suffering from concussion. It was all too much for her to absorb at once. She sensed he was dangerous, but in what way she had no idea. She wanted to leave, quickly, to find Uncle Craig and discover what madness had been happening. She should have let the driver wait, as he had offered, but it was too late now.

'Which hospital is he in?' she asked. 'I'm going to phone for a taxi.'

'There is no need,' the man said, 'I will take you in my car.'

She replaced the receiver slowly. It was essential to keep calm, or at least to appear so. What if he were lying? If he had harmed Uncle Craig, and then taken over the house—*not expecting anyone else to appear*? Before she got into any car with him—before she even moved away from the telephone, she needed some proof that would reassure her. She took a deep breath. She would not show any fear. She must not.

'That is kind of you.' He didn't look kind. He

looked as though he most definitely found her presence disturbing. 'But I wouldn't put you to the trouble. Is he in Esslemont hospital?' She had made the name up. If he said yes, of course, she would *know* he was lying, and she would make some excuse as he went to the car, that she had to go to the loo, anything, and would phone the police.

He frowned. 'No. The name of the hospital is the Kincraig Infirmary.' She felt herself relax slightly. He had stumbled over the unfamiliar words, but they were real, it was genuine, and logical that he would have gone there, for it was ten miles away past Drummell village and before the next town.

'How did he get concussion?' she asked.

'He fell off the high ladder in his library. I was here, I heard the crash, and went in. He was not unconscious, in fact he insisted that he was all right, but when I helped him up, I knew that he needed medical attention and so I made him give me the name of his doctor.' He paused. 'Dr MacFadden, I think was the man who came?'

Victoria let out a little sigh. Yes, she knew Dr MacFadden as well.

'Then—please, can we go?' she asked. She hadn't even taken her coat off yet. She was ready. She began to walk towards the door, and another question struck her. 'How long ago did this happen?' she asked.

'Four days ago—two days after I arrived.' It explained something—but it didn't answer every question. It explained possibly why she hadn't heard, as expected, from her uncle. But it did not explain why this man was here—and apparently so much at home, as if a long-awaited guest, when she, who knew her uncle so well, and knew all of his friends, if not personally, at least by name—had never heard of him. And surely, when the invitation from her uncle had arrived, he would have mentioned that there would be a third person there?

She had to pass near him as he opened the door wider for her and she had to repress the shudder that nearness brought. He *was* like Peter. Taller, bigger, and, with his Slavic features, definably foreign, but the resemblance though faint, was there, and—painful. She passed him. She walked along the wide corridor that only minutes before she had gone along expecting to surprise her uncle asleep over a book. The surprise instead had been hers. And the shock.

They reached the hall and here he took out a bunch of keys from his pocket. She sensed that something, disturbing, from him. And in a minute she was going to get into a car with him, to sit in close proximity for yet another journey, and the thought was a disconcerting one. He was a puzzling man. He didn't speak. He waited for her to go out, and then locked the door behind them, and in that small but proprietorial gesture was a whole world. It was as if he belonged here, and she the interloper.

'Where is your car?' she asked, and he turned, looked down at her, and it was too dark now to see his expression, and perhaps that was fortunate.

'Round the back, in the courtyard,' he replied. 'It is better you wait here I think,' and he strode away before she could say anything, even had she been sure what she would answer. He had a disconcerting effect on her. So she waited, questions seething in her brain. And waited—then heard the sound of a car, and the next moment the blaze of headlights illuminating the trees, casting dark, rapidly moving shadows as he approached. The car drew to a halt, she heard the front passenger door click open—at her side, and he leaned over. It was a large Mercedes, she couldn't see the colour except that it was dark, and it was clearly a left-hand drive model, which told her little save that he must have brought it with him from abroad. Abroad—where? Surely not Russia? She slid in to cushioned warmth and fastened the seat belt. As if it had reminded him, he did the same, then they were moving forward slowly towards the long familiar drive.

It was time for the questions that had been jostling inside her. 'Have you known Uncle Craig for long?' she asked.

'I had never met him before six days ago,' was the level response. He neither looked at her nor added to that startling statement, concentrating on the smoothly curving driveway that stretched before them, and Victoria clutched tightly at her bag, then dared a glance at him, stunned.

He had a hard profile. He seemed unaware of her shock—or uninterested. His eyes were on the road, his hands were on the wheel, and in the light thrown back from the trees that hard implacable outline seemed quite sinister. Dear lord, what did she say next? 'Then—how——' she had to clear her throat, 'did you come to be here? This isn't an hotel.' It seemed stupid, even as the words came out; she couldn't help herself.

This time there was the briefest flicker of a

glance, no more. 'No, I am aware of that. I had a letter of—introduction——' again the slight stumbling over an unfamiliar word, each syllable carefully spaced, his voice very deep. She shivered.

'From—whom?' she managed. She thought letters of introduction were something that had gone out with Victorian bustles, and silver salvers. He *was* like something out of another world.

'From my father. He is an old friend of your uncle.' She didn't know whether she believed him. She didn't know what she believed any more. They had reached the gateway now, and he slowed, waited, and turned to the right on the main road. Fields stretched away on their left, on the right, the walls of Drummell House, and all around them, silence. No houses, no cars, nothing. They could have been in the middle of nowhere.

He drove well, rather fast, but Victoria checked her belt surreptitiously and tried to relax, as the fields sped past. A car approached, in the distance—her first sign of civilisation since she had met Gregor, and as it neared, both dipped their headlights, and she watched it pass, and felt strange, but she wasn't sure why. Then—moments later, she knew. She was used, in whatever situation she found herself, to being told people's entire life stories. It had happened again only an hour or so ago in the taxi travelling from Aberdeen. In a funny way, she had almost come to expect it, and as she found people interesting generally, never minded. But now, here in yet another car, the reverse was happening. When she, who never had to ask, desperately wanted to know, she was having to wrest every word from this stranger, this alien, disturbing man who caused her heart to twist at memories better buried. It disorientated her, making her feel that she was an interloper, a feeling so alien that she couldn't grasp it fully. She had never felt like this before, and certainly not at Drummell House, her second home. Uncle Craig was a huge cuddly bear of a man, her father's older brother by twenty years, and in his home she had always been wanted and welcomed, and cherished. It was he who had taught Victoria about books, who had infected her at an early age with his boundless enthusiasm for the printed word, who treated her like the daughter he had never had, and whom she loved dearly. Their mutual love of books had been one reason why he had invited her to stay only two weeks previously. He had at long last—after Victoria had almost given up hope of persuading him—decided to catalogue and index his vast library, with a view to disposing of some and, she suspected secretly, giving him a chance to add more when the dust had settled. He travelled all over the world, his other pet hobby being philately, and on several occasions Victoria and her sister Anne had travelled with him. She had wonderful memories. . . .

He was speaking, and she realised that she had been miles away. 'I'm sorry?' she said.

'I said, we are nearly there. But in this darkness I am not sure of the road we take now.'

'Oh. Er—next left I think, yes, there's the hospital sign.' The village was not large, a main street, several smaller ones branching off, a couple of pubs, and a hotel, that was all. He turned the car smoothly left, and she looked at the small houses with lighted windows behind which people would be watching their televisions, secure in their little worlds, uncaring, unknowing that she, Victoria Mitchell, was feeling more than a little confused.

The hospital building was even more brightly lit, several cars already parked at the side. Infirmary was rather a grand word for what was in reality a small hospital, and Victoria unfastened her seat belt as Gregory drew to a halt next to a Mini. She opened her door and slid out impatient to see her uncle. Gregor had said that there was no cause for concern, but she had to know for herself, had to ask so many questions—and alone. Which made it the more of a jolt, when, even as those thoughts crossed her mind, Gregor, walking beside her into the brightly lit entrance, opening the door for her, said: 'I shall wait outside your uncle's room while you speak privately to him.'

'Yes—thank you.' Up a flight of stairs, along a yellow-painted corridor, then, for a brief moment, he touched her arm.

'This one I think.' He looked through the glass-topped door. 'Yes, he is there. I shall wait here.' And he sat down on a chair, gave her an impassive glance then looked away towards an approaching nurse who was staring at them both.

'Have you come to see Mr Mitchell?' the nurse, no more than eighteen, asked in her broad Scots accent.

'Yes. Is it all right to go in?' asked Victoria.

'Aye, fine. You can both go.' She looked at Gregor, who smiled at her. Victoria was aware of two things simultaneously. The effect of that smile on the nurse, who blushed prettily—and the difference it made to his face. He had not once smiled at her. She pushed open the door and went in quickly. The room had two beds in, one unoccupied, the other with her uncle, fast asleep. She tiptoed forward and sat quietly down. The television was on, a comedy programme, loud audience laughter wafting out, on her uncle's lap several newspapers. He lay back, snoring gently, oblivious to it all, and Victoria smiled to herself, more in relief than anything. He looked extremely well, only the lack of pillows betraying the concussion. The television was to one side of the bed, angled so that he could presumably see it whilst lying flat. She crept over and switched it off and instantly came that well-loved voice: 'Hey! I was watching that!' and she turned smiling, and Uncle Craig was staring at her, bemused.

'Victoria?' he sounded as if he didn't believe his eyes. 'Is that *you*?' She bent over and kissed him. His white beard tickled her chin. He was like a huge, helpless Father Christmas in pyjamas.

'It's really me,' she answered. 'And you weren't watching it at all, you were fast asleep.'

'Hmm, well, perhaps I was,' he agreed, a broad smile coming on his face. 'Anyway, I don't want to watch now. But my dear girl, how on earth did *you* get *here*?'

She sat down again so that he could see her without moving his head, and took hold of his hand. 'Yes, well,' she began, 'it's a long story, but your visitor brought me——'

'But you came all the way from *London*! How did you know I was in hospital?' His bright blue eyes showed bewilderment.

'Had you forgotten you'd invited me up?' she said softly.

He frowned, then closed his eyes. 'Oh my lord,' he whispered. 'Oh my darling girl—of course I had! What must you have thought when you arrived?'

That would take a book to tell you, she thought. Instead she said: 'Don't worry, love. The concussion probably knocked it out of your head——' she realised what she had said when he started laughing, a little creakily but nevertheless a laugh.

'Oh! I'm sorry,' she began, then started to laugh as well. 'That was an unfortunate choice of words—but Uncle, how soon will you be out?' The next question concerned Gregor Shenkov, and she waited for his reply, so that she could ask it.

'They say in a few days, all being well. And especially if *you're* there—my dear, I had completely forgotten! I'm so sorry——'

'Don't. Just don't worry. I'm there now. But——' and here it came. 'I'm not sure what *he's* doing there.'

Craig Mitchell gave a deep sigh. 'Oh deary me. I'll bet you had a shock, eh?'

'Well—yes,' she admitted.

He chuckled, and squeezed her hand. 'Ah, my dear. There's a tale. I've known Gregor's father for years—never met *him* until the other day— when he turned up out of the blue, and delighted I was to have him, I can tell you! If it hadn't been for him when I fell——' he paused, and Victoria shuddered.

'No, don't think about it. He *was*. Anyway Mrs Holt would have——'

'No, she's away. Got a daughter having a baby, Aberdeen, gone to stay with her for a couple of weeks, see, that's why it was ideal you coming up, company for your aged uncle d'you see? I knew we'd manage splendidly without her—then, anyway, where was I? Oh yes, well Gregor arrived and I thought, ah yes, I'd phone you just to check your trains, he could meet you in Aberdeen, and I was going to—it's all coming back to me now, but we got talking and bless me if one day hadn't passed, then another—and wham! there I was spreadeagled on the library carpet and him picking me up, I remember that, then next thing I'm in here, and after that I don't remember much. He's been every day to see me, good fellow, you'll get along well with him, mind, could be a bit embarrassing just the two of you but you're a sensible girl——'

'Uncle, how long is he staying?' she interrupted desperately.

'Oh. My poor head.' Her uncle winced, and, fearful, Victoria rose to her feet.

'Shall I get a nurse?'

'No! It's nothing. Just a twinge. I have to keep fairly quiet—well, I enjoy the telly as you know so I said blow that, I'm watching Coronation Street, concussion or no—what did you say?'

'It doesn't matter. The main thing is, you'll be home soon.' She must not upset him. She would move into a hotel in the morning, until her uncle was better. The one in the village would be ideal. Let Gregor Shenkov stay at Drummell on his own. There is no way, she decided, that I am going to stay there alone with him. And she looked at her uncle, resolution made, and smiled warmly at him, bent to kiss his forehead, and said: 'I'll get him in,' and turned towards the door. Too late, even as she opened it, she remembered one more question. What on earth had all those books, *in Russian*, being doing there?

CHAPTER TWO

THE journey back to Drummell House would have been accomplished in virtual silence were it not for the taped music Gregor played on the car stereo, and during it Victoria was able to think. It had been obvious, during the time that the Russian had been in the room with her uncle, that the older man had a certain warm respect for the younger one. Virtual strangers they might be, but the link with Gregor's father was clearly an old and valued one. And Gregor himself had been courteous and caring, asking Uncle Craig if there was anything he needed bringing on the following day; he had only to ask. . . .

And then, the visit over, they had left. They had been there half an hour, by which time it was clear that Craig Mitchell was tired. The two men had shaken hands, after which Gregory had said his goodbyes and gone out to wait in the corridor. Victoria, knowing that any more questions would put a strain on the older man, had kissed him, told him she would be in to see him the following day, and left him, one last wave, a kiss blown from the doorway, and she had rejoined the waiting man outside.

They were nearing Drummell House when Gregor switched off the cassette and said: 'Have you had food recently?'

'Not since lunchtime,' she answered.

'Then we shall dine upon our return.' He turned

smoothly into the driveway, through the huge wrought iron gates that Victoria had never seen closed, and along the densely wooded drive.

'And tomorrow I shall go and stay at the hotel in the village so as to be near my uncle until his return home,' she added.

'I see.' What had she expected him to say? 'No—do stay, you have more right than me?' or: 'Why should you do that?' Neither. Instead, the flat, expressionless: 'I see.' He didn't seem to want her there any more than she wanted him, which, perversely, Victoria found annoying. She turned to look at him, and at that precise moment he glanced at her. She could not see the expression on his face, it was too dark in the car, but a brief kind of awareness, an acknowledgment, was exchanged. She shivered inwardly. It was not hostility she felt, it was something far more subtle and strange than that. He doesn't like me, she thought. Perhaps he's a woman hater. And then she remembered the smile at the nurse, the one which had caused her to blush—and she felt brief confusion.

He stopped, at last, outside the entrance, and she slid out, closing the car door after her, and heard the locks click. Then he strode to the front door, keys rattling, and opened it. The warmth from the dying fire hit them. It was extremely cold outside. Cold enough for snow, Victoria thought fleetingly, and then forgot.

Inside the hall he turned to her. 'If you will excuse me, I will go and prepare dinner, unless you would like me to carry your cases upstairs now?'

'I'll only need my small overnight case, *as I'm not staying*,' she answered, warming her hands at the glowing log embers, and looked at him as she spoke and wanted to add—what are you doing here?

'Then—excuse me. I eat in the kitchen. It is easier.'

'That suits me.' She picked up her small case. 'I'll come down when I've washed.'

He turned and walked away without another word. Victoria watched him go. At least he didn't walk like Peter. He moved with an easy grace that belied his size, soft footed, almost silent. Peter had always erupted into rooms, Peter wouldn't know how to walk quietly if he was barefooted, Peter— she shook herself to rid herself of the pain of memory. Sometimes she still ached for him, in those brief moments before sleep when her defences were down, and sometimes she dreamed of him and then when she woke, tears were drying on the pillow. She took a deep breath and went out of the hall and up the stairs, along the familiar corridor to her room.

There she stood at the window for a few moments looking out across the dark vastness surrounding Drummell House. A few hours ago she had felt as though she were coming home again, had thought to see Uncle Craig sitting by a fire with his beloved books scattered around him. Instead, an alien, a dark stranger from another place, another world, looked at her and asked who *she* was, and reminded her only too painfully of things she was trying to forget. She would not forgive Gregor that, even though he would never know.

She flung her case on the bed, opened it and began to take out her toilet bag. Only one night here alone, then a hotel until her uncle returned. It would be easier then. The house was large enough and Gregor would surely not stay long. How long had he been there? Six days? Strangers didn't impose—even if they were the sons of old and valued friends—for more than a week. But perhaps Gregor was not a man who worked by normal, conventional rules, and what was he doing with all those books? That question intrigued Victoria more than anything. It was as if he had come to work, and was in the middle of some enormous task. She would find out, before she went.

After a wash, and make-up, she felt better. Everything would look different in the morning, it always did after a good night's sleep. She snapped her case shut and went down to see what this stranger had prepared to eat.

Delicious smells came from the kitchen. She lifted her head and sniffed appreciatively as she neared it. Was that chicken she could detect? No matter, her stomach protested, and she realised she was extremely hungry. As she went in he turned round from the stove. He wore, wrapped round his waist, one of Mrs Holt's amply sized frilly aprons, and he could have looked comical, but he didn't. He looked every inch a chef. Pans bubbled, steam rose, he had a wooden spoon in his hand. He looked at home. The merest flicker of a smile touched his mouth as he saw the direction of her glance, at the apron, as he too looked down.

'It is nearly ready,' he told her. 'Please be seated.' The long kitchen table was set for two. Victoria obeyed, too bemused to demur. There was, after all, nothing illogical in anything he said, or did. He *was* at home here, in a strange way, and she the new arrival; her uncle had clearly welcomed him warmly and established a rapport with this son of an old friend in the brief days before she came, and if Mrs Holt was away he had very probably taken over the cooking—he certainly seemed to know what he was doing, no doubt about that. Victoria, sitting silently in her place at table, watched him as he stirred something in a large skillet from which arose mouthwatering aromas which combined with others to produce in her something like pain, certainly anticipation. Her uncle had no sense of time when it came to his books or stamps, and if it were left to him, a plate of cheese and biscuits, washed down with a glass or two of wine, was totally acceptable fare. Victoria had stayed on more than one occasion when Mrs Holt had been on holiday and she had cheerfully accepted the fact that if she wanted to eat, she would have to do it herself, and as cooking was one of her many hobbies, she had been happy to do so. And on those occasions, she and Uncle Craig had also eaten in the kitchen, because it was cosy, extremely old fashioned with the huge Aga cooker, the vast sink, the old clock ticking away on the wall, the hard tiled floor scattered with thick—easily washable—rugs, whereas the dining room had an austere formality about it, fine for large dinner parties but impractical for two. Only, now, it wasn't the same any more. Perhaps it never would be again.

Gregor was bending now, taking a roasting dish out, putting it on top, draining off some of the juices in the skillet. The chicken—she had been right about that—was crispily golden. Her stomach gave a silent hollow rumble of protest and she looked down at the table, hands clenched. 'It will be only a minute now,' he said, without turning, and she looked up. Had he read her mind? Did he *know*?

'Shall I get wine or anything?' she asked.

'It is already in the refrigerator,' he answered. 'It is not necessary for you to do anything.' Polite but dismissive, his accent was more pronounced over long words, slower, heavier. The back of her neck tingled in sharp and sudden awareness. She had never met a Russian before, had, after seeing occasional Soviet diplomats interviewed on television, assumed them to be a race lacking in humour, had found the Russian writers she had read somewhat heavy going—they were of a different culture altogether. And this one was more; he was a complete enigma. Perhaps Uncle Craig had seen something she had not. . . .

'Shall I get plates?' she asked desperately.

'They are here.' As he spoke, he produced them from the deep warming tray at the side, and she saw, in almost light-headed relief, that the moment had arrived. His actions were quick and sure; she watched in fascination as wafer thin slices of crisp potato were followed on to plates by carrots and cabbage and finally the chicken, swiftly cut, to be covered in that marvellous mixture from the skillet. The aroma of garlic teased her nostrils, and when he set the plate before her she stared at it, then at him, all resentment for the moment forgotten as she said:

'This looks wonderful!'

'Then eat.' He bowed his head briefly in a grave acknowledgment, opened a bottle of white wine, and poured two glasses full. She needed no instruction for that. The first forkful of chicken was a dream, the second even better. Whatever he was, whoever he was, one thing was certain; he was a culinary wizard. He ate slowly, and sipped his wine, and watched her, and his eyes were sea green, an unusual and striking shade; remote, and the light from above slanted on to his face, adding depth to the cheekbones, the strong hard features, and she sensed infinite power, awesome. She sensed such intensity that it was almost physical, such complexity as she had never before encountered. No, that first fleeting impression had been mistaken. He was not like Peter, for Peter had no depths, Peter had been shallow—and in that realisation, one of the fetters snapped, and it was a kind of brief release. She took a deep breath, and he said: 'It is to your liking?'

She was leaving in the morning. It might be better if she left tonight, but she didn't know why. Her friends didn't disturb her; she could relax with them, enjoy their company, knowing they all shared the same wavelength. She had made a bad mistake with Peter, but no one was perfect. This man disturbed her, *and she didn't know why.* 'It is superb,' she answered. She felt as disorientated as she had when he had first entered the drawing room, a medieval man from another world, another age, and she was having to fight for control. And she succeeded. 'I don't know what it's called, but everything tastes wonderful.'

'The sauce was created by my father. He has a hotel and restaurant a few kilometres outside Paris. I am one of the few people who know the recipe, and when I was coming here, I brought many things, for my father told me that your uncle is a man who appreciates good food.' He raised his glass and drank. 'Your good health.'

'And yours.' Slightly stunned—he had actually *told* her something without being asked—Victoria looked at him wide-eyed, and said the next, ridiculous thing that came into her head: 'But—did you cook it all for yourself? You didn't know I'd be here!' She could have kicked herself. There were so many other questions she could have asked, but there was something so formidable about him that he inhibited her.

'I would have eaten the rest tomorrow.' He didn't seem amused, not quite. Perhaps he already regretted telling her what he had. She didn't know any more. She never needed to ask anyway; people *told* her everything. Only *he* didn't.

'I see.' And before she could even frame another reasonable question, he spoke.

'The hotel where you go to stay tomorrow, do you wish to telephone them first?'

'It won't be necessary. They'll hardly be full at this time of year.' The subject had been changed. Swiftly, painlessly but quite definitely, and she found it sufficiently annoying to enable her to say: 'What is the name of your father's hotel? I may know it.'

'You have been to France?'

'Several times.' She met his eyes now. She was able to. Damn it, why should she let *him* intimidate her? *He* was the outsider, not she. This was her second home, and a much-loved one. He had never even been anywhere near it until less than a week ago. His own eyes regarded her very levelly, yet his voice gave nothing away when he answered:

'*Le Moulin*. There is a water-mill there. It is a very old building.'

'And how long has he been there?'

'At the mill? Fifteen years. In Paris, over twenty years.'

'And before that—where did you live?'

'Near Moscow. I was very young when we—left there.' No mistaking the slight hesitation before those last words. No mistaking his expression either, his eyes bleak and remote. And she sensed she must ask no more, not then at least. 'I will take you if you wish to your hotel tomorrow.'

'That's kind of you.' And then what will you do? Come back here and get on with your research—if that is what it is? But she asked that question only in her mind. She forked up the finely grated cabbage. She had never tasted it like that before, so fine as to be almost minced—with melted butter enriching the taste, almost sweet. Was this then how he ate when he was alone? Like a king? Small clues already gathered were building up a picture, a very incomplete one, but in a few hours, quite a lot. He was wealthy, or apparently so. He drove a very expensive Mercedes, his father owned a hotel and restaurant near Paris, and perhaps Gregor worked there too. The registration plates on the car were certainly the Parisian ones. He was a superb chef. He spoke good English, and undoubtedly French. He was a large powerful-looking man—and he made her feel uncomfortable. Victoria wasn't used to that sensation with anybody. Loved and cherished and part of a closely knit family, her confidence and self-assurance had never been tested—except perhaps over the Peter debacle—and that was as though it had never been as far as her family and close friends were concerned. They never referred to him. It was as though he had never existed. Better that way. Or was it? This man, without even realising it, had made her question it.

'I must phone my parents!' she thought, horrified at realising they wouldn't know about Uncle Craig, and it was only when he replied that she realised she had spoken her thoughts out loud.

'Then go now. I have made no pudding. There is fresh fruit.'

She looked up, startled, from her empty plate, then stood. 'Yes, of course. They might have been trying to phone me while we were out.' And what if they had telephoned later, and Gregor had answered? What would they make of him?

She crossed the hall. Gregor must have replenished the fire while she was upstairs. It glowed more lively, and her suitcases had been placed in a corner out of the way. Along that familiar corridor, not quite the same now, into the drawing room. There too, the fire blazed, and the books had been stacked neatly closed on the table near the fireplace. He must be a quick worker, she thought. All that and dinner too. She picked up the telephone and began to dial.

Victoria went early to her bedroom taking several books with her. And there, at last, she felt at home. It had been her room for as long as she could remember, even when, as a child, she had come up with parents, sister Anne and brother Michael. A large, high-ceilinged room with a warm electric fire and her own choice of pictures on the walls, it welcomed her. She settled down in bed,

hot water bottle at her feet, door bolted—she had
never done that before, never needed or wanted to.
But now she was truly alone and more than a little
tired after a long train journey. She had spoken to
her father on the telephone first, and after telling
him about his brother Craig, and assuring him
that there was no cause for concern, had then told
him about Gregor. Yes, he had heard of Craig's
Russian friend—Ivan might be his name, her
father thought, and what a good job the son had
been there when it happened. Victoria had had to
repress a smile at that. No parental concern about
his beloved younger daughter being ensconced
with a total stranger, no questions about him!
Which was typical of her father, who, in his own
way, was as delightfully impractical as his older
brother. She had promised to phone again when
Craig came home, and that had been that.

Comfortable, she lay back and began to read,
but soon the words danced on the page, the lines
blurred and ceased to make sense. She lay the
book aside, switched off the light and turned to
face the window. The moon had a hazy ring round
it in a pale dark sky, several stars glittered, bright
diamonds in infinity, and the house was silent. She
did not know how near Gregor's room was, the
thick carpets throughout the house effectively
deadened sound. But he was somewhere, whether
up or down. He was *there*. He was a man it would
be very difficult to ignore. Just before she drifted
into sleep came the image of him as he had
appeared in the doorway, quite startling, never to
be forgotten, that first impression.

She slept, and dreamed of him riding a white
horse, dressed in medieval clothes, a magnificent

man on a magnificent beast riding across snowy wastelands with stark black trees outlined sharply against a bleak Siberian sky. A man with startling green eyes who turned and looked at her as she rode beside him, and the image changed and became Peter and she stirred restlessly in her sleep, knocking the book to the floor, which woke her. Startled, she sat up, thinking that Gregor had come into her room, but there was no one, and when she switched on the light, the door was securely bolted. She turned the lamp off and lay down, the aftertaste of the dream lingering for a while as she watched the window and saw soft snowflakes drifting down silently past the panes. There was something so soothing and hypnotic about the sight that she drifted away as easily as the flakes fell, and this time there were no dreams for a while. None that disturbed at any rate. . . .

She woke up some hours later refreshed after a deep sleep, and light filled the room. The light from the snow, and curious to see it, always having loved it, she went to the window as she had done so often as a child in winter and saw to her delight that everything was white outside, the earth blanketed, trees outlined darkly—but she had forgotten the dream. And the significance of the snow did not strike her. Not then.

Victoria looked at her bedside clock. It showed just after six. She thought she might not sleep again, and, putting on her dressing-gown, padded silently out along the corridor. A drink of hot chocolate seemed to be the most pleasant idea, and she would sleep again afterwards. Down the stairs, along a silent corridor, through a silent hall, fire dead, into the kitchen, milk from the refrigerator, powdered chocolate in cupboard, milk in pan, warming.... She went over to the window, stirring the chocolate with a teaspoon of milk in the beaker. The silent world greeted her through the window. The snow fell thicker now, huge soft flakes clinging to the window, sliding, falling. Beautiful. She was only half awake. She laid her palm on the glass, and several large flakes melted and vanished into drops that winked in the light, and she smiled to herself, and she still didn't realise what was happening. She didn't realise until she woke up the second time at ten o'clock. And then, it was too late.

It was Gregor who woke her by knocking on her door. Startled, she called: 'Just a moment,' snatched her dressing-gown off the chair and went to unbolt the door.

He stood outside, dressed as he had been the day before. But the expression on his face was what held her. 'What is it?' she said, her first thought of Uncle Craig.

'Come downstairs. I will show you,' he answered, and turned away. She followed and he went across the hall and opened the front door. And then, at last, she knew what she should have known when she had gone down to make the hot chocolate. Stunned, she stared out at the white wilderness—the snow—chest high outside the door, his car half submerged, and her eyes widened in horror. She turned to him, unable to speak. His eyes said what she could not. 'We cannot get out. You cannot leave today to go to your hotel, Victoria.'

'But I can't stay!' she gasped.

He looked down at her, towering over her, she

feeling uncomfortably small, feeling the sharp bite of the cold air filling her. 'You have no choice,' he said flatly, and closed the door again. 'Come, we had better eat. There is food in the kitchen. I have taken the radio out there.'

She walked away, he following, and the kitchen was warm, and a kettle bubbled on the stove. She looked towards the window, and the faint imprint of her hand could be seen, and she remembered what she had done. If she had known, then, and had woken him, it would not have been too late. But it was now. She shivered. 'I don't want to stay,' she said.

He did not answer. He went to the kettle and took it off the hot plate and filled two beakers. When he had handed her one he sat down opposite her. His next words caused her to nearly drop her beaker of coffee, so startling and unexpected were they. 'Who is Peter?' he asked.

Victoria froze. She had not heard him correctly. She *could not have*.

'What did you say?' she whispered, and she felt as if all the blood had drained from her face, and clutched the table.

'I think you have already answered me.'

'No—*tell me what you said again*.'

'I asked you—who is Peter?' In the background, pop music from the radio, not loud, but crystal clear in that sudden silence.

'What made you say that?'

'When I arrived—a week ago—and your uncle answered the door, he said—before I had time to speak, you understand, "Good grief—it's Peter"—and I said—"Mr Mitchell, my name is Gregor Shenkov, I am the son of Ivan——" and then he answered—"Ah, for a moment I thought—my God! Ivan's son——"' He paused. His eyes were very steady on her white face. 'Later, when we had spoken for some time, and I asked him if he had mistaken me for someone, he told me—that Peter was the name of a friend of one of his nieces——'

'No!' Victoria jumped to her feet. She didn't want to hear. She had taken Peter there, once only, for a long weekend. They had flown from London to Aberdeen. She had wanted to show Peter her second home—but it had been a mistake. Shaking, she stood facing him, aghast at her own behaviour. This should not have happened. Taking a deep breath she said: 'It doesn't matter now. Peter was someone I once knew.' And that is all you need to, or are going to know, she added to herself.

'But it explains now, to me, your reaction when I walked in,' he said softly.

My reaction when I first saw you, just for a moment, was that I had strayed into another world, another time, she thought, still recovering from the startler that had been as intense as a blow to her heart. Her breathing was returning to normal. In a second she would *be* normal again. '*My* reaction,' she said at last, calmly, or nearly so, 'was one of shock, because I thought you were my uncle—only you weren't.'

She moved smartly away from the table and yanked a slice of toast from the toaster, and buttered it with fierce concentration. Damn him. Why did he have to ask that? She didn't feel hungry. She didn't want the toast—she wanted to leave. Only she couldn't.

'Am I like *him*?' His words made her turn, slowly, and Gregor rose to his feet and came from the table to her, and she flinched in an instinctive reaction that she could no longer help. She felt weak and afraid—she felt——

'No,' she whispered. 'Please—no.' And Gregor stopped, near her, a foot or so away, as if her words had been an amulet. She didn't look at his face, she couldn't. She put the toast down on a plate, concentrating on that, willing him to go away, to leave her alone with her hurt. Tears stung at the backs of her eyes, and she blinked hard and swallowed. For a few intense moments neither moved nor spoke, a frozen tableau, and then he broke the spell by turning away again, going over to the radio and turning it louder. He had heard what she had not, the voice of the announcer cutting in with a weather report—'Heavy snow has fallen overnight in the north east of Scotland,' she listened to the words, not fully concentrating on them, they were hollow sounds filling the room, that was all—'most roads are impassable. Motorists are advised that outside the larger cities——' on and on, a meaningless jumble that told her only one thing. There was no way that either of them could leave Drummell House for the next few days, unless a miracle happened. The bulletin finished. She was aware of him turning the sound down, aware of his movements, aware, at last, that he was speaking to her, and she looked up at him then.

'What did you say?' she asked.

'I said that I am going to make sure we have a good supply of logs. And while I am doing so, it would be sensible if you telephone the hospital and explain to your uncle——'

'Yes, of course.' Safe now, safer anyway. Different topics. 'The wood is kept in the old stables across the courtyard at the back.'

'I know. I have already been over there this morning. I had to dig my way across.' She noticed then what she had not before, that Gregor wore no shoes, and that a large pair of wellingtons stood by the door leading to the kitchen passage to the back. In a way it made her feel a little ashamed. She had been sleeping, blissfully unaware, and he had been working already. At times of emergency, as this was—and she had been here previously when the world came to a standstill in snow—it was necessary for everyone to pull their weight. And she knew other things that he did not. Better to say them now. 'I had best tell you. It is possible that the power will go off. Snow affects the pylons sometimes——'

'Your uncle told me that. You know where the lamps are kept?'

'Yes. I will get them ready. Also candles.'

'Then we are prepared for whatever happens.'

Are we? she thought. I wonder. But all she said was: 'Yes. I'll phone first.' She picked up her toast and coffee and went out. Already the change in temperature was obvious as she crossed the hall. The central heating was oil fired, and the radiators were warm to the touch, but it was not enough. In really extreme conditions, when winter bit hard, Uncle Craig had been known to live entirely in the main drawing room, keeping a blazing log fire going day and night, and closing the upper floor entirely. Yet it would never have occurred to him to leave Scotland in the harsher months of the year. His books were too precious to leave, he said, and always kept another fire going in his library. Mrs Holt, his widowed elderly house-keeper, was as tough as him, and would have scorned any other way. Victoria smiled to herself at the memories as she picked up the telephone. The line was crackling, and it took several attempts to get through to the hospital, but she managed at last. She gave the ward sister her messages, was assured that Mr Mitchell was much better, that, clearly, he would not be able to leave hospital in any event until the roads were passable, and that the snow was just as bad there. She hung up, feeling suddenly flat. One day more, one day later, and she would not have been able to make it. She would have been stranded in Aberdeen and could have stayed with friends there, would have telephoned, and got Gregor—but she was here instead, and likely to be so for some time. Overnight, everything had become startlingly changed. The world was a different place. And Gregor knew about Peter. That was, in a strange way, the most disturbing thing of all.

CHAPTER THREE

VICTORIA had a warm shower, then dressed in the old jeans and grey sweater that she kept at Drummell House. There was work to be done while it was daylight, in case. . . .

She found five paraffin lamps and left them in the kitchen together with the huge box of candles and a torch, put on her wellingtons and old mac from the back door, and opened it to see a clear but narrow track in the snow leading to the stables where the paraffin was stored. She could hear the sound of chopping emerging from the open stable door and made her way across. The snow was still falling, not as heavily, but steadily, and about four foot deep. The air was crystal clear, the snow dazzling to her eyes. She entered the comparative gloom of the large stable and paused in the doorway. Gregor had his back to her, at the chopping bench, his arms rising and falling in rhythmic movements as he axed the wood into logs. She watched silently for a few moments, impressed, despite herself, at this evidence—if any were needed—of his strength. A high stack of logs, and a wheelbarrow full, spoke of his industry. He had wasted no time. A pause, and he turned, as if suddenly aware of her presence. Sweat glistened on his face and bare forearms, and she saw his powerful arm muscles. He put the axe down and wiped his forehead as if glad of a break in his labours.

'I've come for the paraffin,' she said. 'Please don't let me disturb you.' He let out his breath in a deep sigh. 'I need a rest,' he admitted wryly.

'Shall I make you a cup of coffee?'

'Yes please.'

'And I'll take the paraffin now. Come in in two minutes, it will be ready.' She lifted the large can nearest to her and went out. Immediately on entering the kitchen she put the kettle on and washed his beaker ready for when he returned. He had done a lot, he deserved a cup of hot coffee at least. He also deserved food. When he walked in, and took off his wellingtons, she said: 'I'll make lunch.'

'Thank you.' He sat at the table, long legs sprawled out, and leaned back in the chair. 'I have more to do. There will be enough then for at least a week. I see you have the lamps.' He touched one, turned the wick experimentally. 'That is good.'

'I came here to work for my uncle. There is no reason why I shouldn't get on with it while he is away. I shall be working in the library, so I shall light a fire there as well,' she told him, without adding the unnecessary words—then we can keep out of each other's hair—and because she had forgotten about his books, which had vanished when she went into the drawing room to telephone, she felt a sense almost of shock when he answered:

'That is where I am working also.'

The coffee was made. She had the beaker in her hand and turned slowly.

'You—are working—in the library?'

'It is why I came,' and he looked steadily at her as she put his coffee on the table.

'To work in my uncle's *library*?' The books—of *course*!—but surely *they* hadn't come from there?

'You are puzzled?' Too damn right I'm puzzled, she thought but didn't say. In a moment her question would be answered. Slowly now, he's not a man who tells anything easily.

'Mildly,' she answered, in magnificent understatement. 'I just didn't know his collection was so well known.'

'Some of my family history is here.' The words themselves were spoken calmly, almost flatly, but Victoria's head jerked back and she looked at him, stunned.

'*Your* family *history?*' she echoed the words. '*Here?*'

'Have I said something so strange?'

'But you are——'

'Russian?' he said the word during her hesitation, and very drily.

'Yes.'

'And I have ancestors who came originally from Scotland. From this north-eastern part of Scotland. Many, many years ago, Victoria——' the way he spoke her name was intriguing. Veek-tor-ya. He made it sound Russian. She almost wanted to hear him say it again. She liked her name, but no one had ever pronounced it quite like that before. His voice was deep, caressing. She wondered how he would speak the words of love, and her spine tingled at the thought, and she watched his hands as he picked up his beaker, strong hands, but sensuous, with long fingers, the nails cut short and square, broad hands, powerful ones too. . . . She caught her breath, not sure what madness was happening to her, she, a sane and sensible woman of twenty-four. . . .

'Yes,' she said desperately. 'I see.' But she didn't. She didn't see at all, and he looked at her oddly, as if he wondered what she was about, and she gave herself a mental shake. 'So that is why—the—er—books were set out in the drawing room.'

'Ah, you saw them? Of course.'

'They are my uncle's books?'

'Some of them, yes.'

'And you didn't want me here because you preferred to work alone?' She was stronger now. Some brief madness had passed, hopefully for good.

'Is that how it seemed?'

'Yes.' She could meet his eyes again. How strange they were, how startling in the impact. Eyes that looked deep into her soul, darkly lashed. He could hypnotise, with those eyes. Stop reading my mind! she thought.

'That was not exactly the reason,' he said. A lock of hair had fallen on his forehead, and he brushed it back, thick glossy black hair growing low in a widow's peak.

'Then what was?' she asked, and he shrugged.

'It is not important.'

'Oh, I see. I'm not expected to ask questions, is that it?' Then she added softly: 'But you can, of course.'

'Because I asked who Peter was?'

'Yes.'

'And you do not wish to talk about him.' It was a statement, not a question.

'No, I don't.'

'Then I will not ask.'

She should have stayed on the subject of his arrival. She didn't know how it had drifted from that on to this dangerous ground. She wasn't sure of anything very much any more. 'I—I'll make myself a coffee I think, and start preparing lunch,' and she hurried away from him and when she put the kettle to her beaker it hit it, and rattled because her hand was not quite steady. She would go mad here with him. The snow would eventually clear but she would be a gibbering wreck. There was a waiting stillness about him. An air of controlled tension as if he too sensed her confusion, and watched, like some jungle predator, to pounce when she was unaware. She filled the beaker with milk. How could she tell him that? Yet it was what she felt. He was watching her with that air of stillness, disturbing her immensely yet in no tangible way. She had known him less than one whole day. It didn't seem possible but it was so. Less than twenty-four hours. And days stretched ahead. By any logic it would be three or four days before roads were passable—and they would be only the main ones.

The sound of his beaker on the table was like a gunshot in the tense silence and she started. Then, he was on his feet, the chair scraping back. He was moving. 'I will go and finish my work.' He had rolled down his sleeves when he had come in. Now, slowly, he rolled them up again, to the elbows, the hard muscular forearms revealed, covered in dark hair. He could crush her if he chose, could take her in those arms and hold her so that she would not be able to move. . . .

'Yes.' It was all she could say. When he had gone she went over to the small mirror on the door and looked at herself. Her face gave nothing away of her inner turmoil, which was a relief. She had rounded cheekbones and a fine clear skin, and wide set gold flecked brown eyes of remarkable innocence that looked out at the world from the safety and cushioned warmth of her secure family background. Her hair was a sunstreaked pale auburn-gold shade, long and silky—she generally tied it back to work—she raised her hand now and smoothed it from her face, and ran her tongue across her lower lip in disturbing memory of an imagined kiss, and quickly turned away from the mirror because she was not reassured by what she had seen. She had had a briefly strange and disturbing thought, and she didn't like it. It must not happen again.

Some of my family history is here. The words lingered in her mind, a shock, as though somewhere a door had opened, and she had caught a glimpse of the past—and brief memory flickered, of that very first impression of him. Had she perhaps—a remote possibility, but she was beginning to think that nothing, however absurd seeming, was impossible—had she perhaps seen a picture of one of Gregor's own ancestors in one of her uncle's books at some time in the past, and had that memory been triggered off by his unexpected appearance?

She went back towards the stove, collected some dirty pans and carried them over to the sink. Filling the bowl with hot water she determinedly emptied her mind of such fancies. This way lies madness, she decided. For the next few days, I am going to cook, and clean, and in between times get down dozens and dozens of dusty books from the library shelves, and occupy myself with sensible, practical things. I will speak politely and civilly to

Comrade Shenkov and learn how to get on with this man with whom I am most unfortunately marooned, and when I eventually get back to London, all this will be a pleasantly amusing little tale to tell to my friends and I shall embroider it slightly and describe him as a somewhat gorgeous giant with raven hair and startling green eyes, and have Anne, and Kath and Debbie and others, positively gnashing their teeth in envy—and then we'll all have a good giggle. . . . She paused in mid scrub with the scourer and stared fixedly out of the window. Embroider it? she thought. If I tell the exact truth, give them a precise description, that will be fantasy enough. Is he real? Am I perhaps the one with concussion, and dreaming all this? Did something happen to me on the way in? And she shivered, because at that moment, there was only a fine dividing line between reality and fantasy. It *was* an unbelievable situation. But it had happened. It was real enough—and so was the snow, piled high on the window ledge. She opened the window, slid it up, and pushed the snow away with her hands. Cold air rushed in and she pulled the window closed again. Her view was now uninterrupted. And what a view it was! The thick tree trunks standing black and stark, sentinels guarding the house, branches heavily laden with snow, the leaden sky threatening yet more, and nothing moving. It was like a still picture frozen in time, unreal yet magnificent. The radio, soft in the background, seemed a last link with reality, certainly the only link with civilisation. How strange it would be if electricity failed, and the telephone. Then there would be no voices from outside entering the house. She shook her head and began to scrub vigorously at the pan. 'I think I'll start with the books nearest the fire in the library,' she said out loud. 'I can move that large table nearer and stack them on that, and keep the file cards on it as well.' That banished the sense of unreality all right. In her mind's eye she could already see everything set out. It would therefore be a good idea to light the fire in the library so that the large room would be warm. She finished the pans, rinsed the bowl out, dried her hands, and went to find newspaper to start the fire.

Late afternoon on a November day, and the world outside settled in for a long night. With the snow, it would never get really dark, there would always be that eerie greyish reflection from the land, but there was the faintest trace of mist as well, making that outside stillness almost a tangible force. Victoria, in the library, paused in her labours and went over to the window, drawn irresistibly by the view, so nearly obscured now in the gloom. Her reflection on the glass was very clear, tall and slender still despite the bulk of her sweater. Thank God for warm clothes, she thought. The light from behind her caught her hair so that it gleamed silky gold, and she moved slightly, and pressed her face to the glass. There was a fairy-tale quality to everything, the snow with a grey ghostly sheen, the guardian trees. Easy to imagine those shadows moving. . . .

She turned away abruptly and the images were shattered, and she looked back to her table, laden with books, and the log fire sending frantic red sparks up the wide chimney. The logs crackled satisfyingly, and shifted and stirred as they burned.

She had been working there for over three hours, and it was time for a break. Her hands and face were grimy with the dust of ancient tomes, and it had made her throat dry. Leaving the library, closing the door behind her, she walked soft footed along the corridor—the library was next to the drawing room, an identical size and shape but so different in atmosphere—and went into the small cloakroom under the stairs to wash hands and face. Here it was cold, as if the central heating was already wilting under the extra burden of heat needed.

Then along, and through the hall—the fire needed replenishing and she bent and placed two more logs on it, dusted her hands on her jeans and went on her way to the kitchen. Gregor was there, preparing dinner as she had known he would be. It had been decided over lunch that she would prepare the midday meal, he the evening one. Breakfast would be on a whoever was up first basis, which suited Victoria admirably. One slice of toast and a cup of coffee was all she usually wanted anyway. He looked up from the table, and there were tears in his eyes—and she saw that he was dicing onions, and repressed a smile.

'I've come for a cup of coffee,' she said. 'Shall I make you one?'

'Please.' He wiped his cheek.

'We may run out of fresh vegetables tomorrow,' she said, filling the kettle. 'But there are ample frozen ones in the freezer.'

'I know. I have already checked everything.' He tipped the tiny squares of onion into a large pan. 'There is also a larder full of tinned and dried food of many varieties. We have no more milk, but there is powdered also in the pantry, and I will make bread tomorrow.'

'You've been busy then,' she remarked, impressed by his efficiency. 'I just hope the electricity doesn't fail.'

He shrugged. 'It will be a minor inconvenience, no more than that.'

She looked at him. A minor *inconvenience*! She opened her mouth to speak, thought better of it, and closed it again, but he saw. He knew. That flicker of awareness touched his eyes. 'We shall still be warm, and we shall eat, and we shall both get on with the work we have decided to do.' His eyes met hers, challenging her. There was an air about him of—not exactly of aggression, more a supreme confidence. Yes, that was it, she decided, in the split second after. He was a superbly self-confident individual, damn him! In an odd way—and she didn't understand why—it irritated her, which she knew was ridiculous, because he spoke sense.

'I've been here before in winter,' she said swiftly, 'and I do *know* what it's like—*and we've* managed too!' A childish answer really, she knew that even as the words came out, but at least it made her feel less irritated with him and his smug superiority.

He raised one eyebrow as he turned away, a dismissive gesture, and she added hotly: '*I'd* manage perfectly well without *you*!'

He turned back. 'Did I say you would not?' he said, voice deceptively soft, for there was a core of steel there, she could almost *feel* it, and her spine tingled.

'You implied it!' Her cheeks were warm. She wished her skin were not so fair, so transparent. He would see.

'Your imagination is too vivid, I think. It would be better if you made the coffee you have offered me, and then went back to your books,' and he turned away again and bent to the vegetable drawer as though the subject was closed. *He* had spoken. Victoria could have *hit* him. Who the hell did he think he was, talking to her as though she was a child! Wide eyed, she stared at him, searching for suitable words to tell him precisely what she thought of him—then, taking a deep breath, she counted to ten. It would be no use. He probably had a hide like an elephant. She pulled a face at him, and the second later he was straightening up, holding a cauliflower from which he proceeded to strip the leaves with an air of such nonchalance that it was almost as if nothing had happened. In a minute he'll start whistling, she thought crossly, and filled the beakers, stirring the coffee powder in with unaccustomed vigour.

'Here is your coffee,' she said, her voice like stone, and he looked at her and answered:

'Thank you. Leave it there.'

She took hers and walked out stiff legged, her back ramrod straight. She felt as if his eyes were on her as she went. Eyes that might be amused. She didn't turn round to find out, merely closed the door decisively after her and returned, thinking dire thoughts, back to the library. Within minutes her normal good humour was restored. She was even able to see an amusing side to the scene. Something to tell the girls, after all. He was simply a Russian male chauvinist pig—clearly a particularly virulent species, she decided. She finished her coffee, picked up the next book, and her file card, and began to write.

The next hour passed quickly. Once she was engrossed in her work nothing else mattered. She might well have been entirely alone in that vast grey stone mansion. She was printing neatly on a card when the lights flickered twice then went out. The room was plunged into darkness, saved only by the firelight dancing on walls and ceiling. For a moment she waited, unbelieving, hoping against hope that this was a temporary fault, that any moment they would come on again as before. Nothing. Victoria stood up and made her way to the door, opened it and began walking along the corridor. Strange how completely different it all was in pitch darkness, every tiny sound intensified, the small distant creaks of ancient wood, the far away tick of a clock. Nearly at the end of the corridor now. She would soon be in the hall, and that would be lit by the fire—and she rounded the corner and the sky fell down and hit her, winding her, knocking every ounce of breath from her body at the impact—and a pair of powerful arms went round her, and a surprised male voice said: 'I was coming to tell you that the meal was ready,' and she disentangled herself from Gregor's arms, and her breathing was unsteady with that mixture of shock and fear she had just experienced.

'Oh!' she gasped, more to let her take breath in than anything else. 'I thought for a moment the roof had fallen in.'

'Did I hurt you?'

'No. I'm just out of breath.' And he hadn't even tried. He had been moving more quickly than she, and the memory of an extremely hard body remained. She wondered quite unconsequentially whether they ever played rugby in the Soviet

Union. He would have made an invaluable prop forward. 'The lights——'

'Yes. Come back to the kitchen. We will light two lamps.' And he took her arm as he turned, and led the way back. Not a heavy grip, his hand resting near her elbow, that was all, but it was more than enough. His touch was warm through the wool of her sweater. It was very warm.

'I can—manage——' she started to say, but he ignored her, and they crossed the hall, and they could see—well, almost—there, but his hand remained, and her skin tingled. Then into the kitchen where, at the table, he released his hold. She had put matches ready. She lit one and the soft yellow flame bloomed like a large candle. Victoria blew the match out before it singed her fingers and lit a second one. He had placed the first lamp right next to the cooker, and she put the other one in the centre of the large table. Was it her imagination or had the room gone colder? 'Can I help you?' she offered. The newest implications were just striking her. It was one thing to theorise on how to cope when the light failed—it was something else to experience it. The water was heated by the central heating system, and the Aga worked by gas, but lights were never fully appreciated until they were gone, and the reality gradually sank in fully. There would be no more indexing except in daylight—even then a lamp was sometimes necessary on a gloomy day. She had been here twenty-four hours that was all, and during that time had become snowbound— and now this. Surely nothing else could happen? It couldn't get worse—or could it? And he turned at that thought, and as if in answer to it, said: 'I regret to tell you this, but the telephone also is not working any more.'

'Oh, *no*!'

'Oh—yes. You may see for yourself, Victoria——' he gestured towards the kitchen extension and she went over to it and picked it up. There was no dialling tone, just an emptiness that echoed back hollowly. She replaced the receiver with a hand that was not quite steady. That was it then. They had nothing. Just themselves. They were dependent on each other now, and would be for—how long? She glanced towards the window and it had started to snow again after a halt of several hours. Silent flakes, silent, *deadly* flakes, blanketing everything around, inexorable, unstoppable. She felt a wrenching sense of despair and put her hand to her mouth to stifle a small cry of utter hopelessness. He heard, turned, looked at her.

'You are frightened?' He wouldn't understand, and how could she tell him?

'*No*. I told you, I've been here before when—this——' she gestured towards the window—'has happened.'

'But with others, your family—your—friends.' Was it her imagination, or did he hesitate before that last word? 'Not with a——' there was a definite pause this time, not imagined, 'a stranger——'

'No.' Her voice was a whisper, no more, her defences down.

'Then we will have to learn to—what is your English expression? To get along with each other, will we not?'

'Yes.'

He did something very suddenly and totally
unexpectedly, came over in one stride to where she
sat, and pulled her to her feet. Victoria gasped in
shock, and he held her arms and looked down at
her, face shadowed, the lamps behind him. 'Then
we shall do so,' he said, the deep voice deeper, the
accent stronger still. 'You are safe with me. You
need have no fear of me in any way.' She knew
what he meant, of course she did. She would have
been a fool not to have wondered that, and she
met his eyes fearlessly now.

'I don't know you, do I?'

'That is why I have told you.' He released her
abruptly. 'I know what must have been in your
mind.' She could feel the imprint of his fingers
through the sleeves, even though he no longer
touched her. 'And as I remind you of someone
who has hurt you——'

'No! You said you wouldn't mention——'

'It is necessary.' His voice cut in, tone decisive.
'Is that how *he* was?'

'No! You don't understand—you can't—I won't
talk about him——'

'Then don't. But I am not like *him*——'

He had got it wrong. Misunderstood, perhaps
deliberately. She was no longer sure of anything.
She felt helpless and confused and she wasn't used
to feeling either of those things. 'No, you're
mistaken. That's not why——' she stopped. She
had nearly fallen into a trap.

'He was married—only he did not tell you?'

Victoria sat down again, her legs suddenly weak.
And she did not answer. She couldn't. Instead the
hot tears came, and she put her head in her hands
to hide them from him, and heard his wordless

exclamation. The next moment his arms were around her. He was crouching beside her, and he held her closely to him, and her sobs were muffled against his shoulder. 'I should not have said that.' His voice was softer now, less hard. She was being lifted to her feet, gentler now, still held. She heard the chair fall backwards, the sound like a gunshot echoing, and she was safe. Strange how she should feel that, with him, very strange. She felt secure and protected. She moved slightly, for he had held her very close, and he moved one hand from her back, and brought it to her face, and lifted her chin up, and she was forced to look at him, even though he was a blur of tears. Then he kissed her.

It was a light kiss, perhaps one of apology for his unconscious cruelty, no more. There was no passion and nothing sexual in it. But it was a wonderful experience, albeit brief; she had never been kissed in such a way before by anyone. Then it was over, and he released her so carefully that there was no sense of loss. And Victoria stood facing him and thought—I shall remember that for as long as I live, and her heart missed a beat, and something quite strange was there, filling the room, and her, as she looked at him. He put a finger on her cheek and smoothed away the tears and his fingers were so soft, the touch like a butterfly's wing, caressing. And she knew that this man was extraordinary. Whatever else she felt about him, resentment perhaps at his being there, his supreme confidence bordering on arrogance— whatever else there was, he was also capable of tenderness. An inward tremor shook her. She didn't want that, or need that from *him*. She did not need his pity. She blinked away the last foolish tears and took a deep breath.

'Yes, he was married,' she said very calmly, as if it were a matter of no great importance. 'But I found out in time, so no damage was done.' How easily a lie came when self-defence was needed! She moved away from him smartly. 'It happens to everyone sometime or another. Don't tell me you've never made a—mistake?'

'Several,' was the dry cryptic answer, 'but then—who has not?'

She sat down at the already laid table again. 'Then you will understand why I prefer the subject to be closed,' she said in flat tones.

'Yes. I do. The meal is ready, Victoria,' the name again, her name, said in that way so very different from anything. 'We will eat, and you will perhaps tell me what it is you are doing in the library?'

'Uncle Craig has decided, after many years of persuasion, to allow his books to be catalogued. I'm listing them all, then going to get them in some kind of order, and no doubt he will want to dispose of some—so that he'll have room for more,' she added. She was even able to smile at that.

'I see.' He put plates on the table, then sat down. She had eaten ratatouille before, and this looked, and smelt, delicious. She began to eat, and it was. 'Then maybe,' he continued as they ate, 'you might be able to help me in my search. No doubt you have a better idea than I where everything is kept?'

'I'm not sure about that. I've never explored all his books. I didn't even know he had any in Russian—but I'll certainly look tomorrow. It's impossible now.'

'He was up the ladder getting some books down for me when he had his accident I regret to say.'

'The ladder is rickety anyway,' she answered. This was a safe subject now. The kiss was almost forgotten, if indeed it had ever happened. She was beginning to wonder if she had imagined it. For strangely, she had thought, long before it happened, had imagined—Deep breath, continue. 'Er—he should have got a new one ages ago. It's a relief that it happened when it did, and you were here. He could well have been up on his own——' she stopped.

'Then perhaps it was,' he cut in. 'One reason I have not attempted to climb it and see for myself. I fear it would not bear my weight.'

I'm darned sure it wouldn't, she thought, having seen the size of you, but all she said was: 'You're probably right. However, I'm a lot lighter than both you and my uncle. In the morning, if you'd like before I start my work, I'll climb up and see what I can find—only I'd prefer it if you held the ladder for me.'

'Of course. To catch you if you fall?' Was that a glimmer of a smile?

'Something like that,' she agreed. It might not be necessary to add that she hated ladders anyway, her only phobia, three steps up and she got vertigo, which was ridiculous, and she was mildly ashamed of this weakness, but she wasn't going to admit it to anyone, certainly not Gregor. Uncle Craig knew, had always known, never teased, and would have done the higher shelves for her anyway. Now, before she reached them, there would be a new ladder. She had a month's accumulated leave from her work as archivist at

London University. A month in Scotland, and then home for Christmas, the perfect antidote to— no, she wasn't going to think of Peter again. Not any more.

'I shall make sure it is secure before I allow you to climb, Victoria——' There it was again, Veek-tor-ya. A little tingle ran down her spine.

Quickly she said: 'This is delicious, Gregor.' It was the first time she had consciously called him by name. She wondered how her pronunciation of it sounded to his ears. 'Do you work with your father at the hotel?'

'No. But it was he—and my mother—who taught me my love of cooking. Now it is something I do for pleasure, but not for work.'

'What is your work?' He could refuse to answer of course. She had sensed a reluctance to talk about himself, but she knew he would not, not now, not after what had happened. . . .

There seemed to be a slight pause, to her sensitive ears anyway. Was he reluctant? She waited, holding her breath, but not aware of doing so. Then he spoke: 'I own a shop in Paris. A sports store—and also one in the French Alps.' And at his words, an awareness, a recognition of the surname came to Victoria.

'You—a *sports* shop? And does it sell skiing equipment?'

He smiled faintly. 'Yes. You have a reason for asking, I think.' A statement, not a question.

'You are a skier, aren't you? A famous one—of *course*. Shenkov! You won a gold medal for France in the last winter Olympics! My God—*was* that *you*?' Her eyes were wide; stunned, Victoria stared at him in sudden recognition, and saw him nod.

'You have a remarkable memory.'

'I watched you on television.' She saw it again in her mind's eye, as vivid and real as it had been then. The leap from the top, that breathtaking, heart-stopping take-off into the air that always caused a wrench of pure terror and awe mingled in her. She who could not climb a ladder, was sitting opposite a man who had leapt into space many times, to weave a magic path down a dizzyingly steep mountainside. She had seen him do so, heard the roars of the crowd, had shared in those few exquisite minutes of poetry in motion—stunned, she could not speak.

CHAPTER FOUR

'I HOPE to go for a few days to Aviemore when I leave here,' said Gregor, with a wry glance towards the window. 'If we ever leave.' He looked again at Victoria. 'Do you ski?'

Perhaps it was time for confession, before—or in case—she made an utter fool of herself on the ladder. 'I can't even go up a ladder without feeling dizzy. And I've never told anyone that before. Your remark about catching me if I fall was more accurate than you realised. I well might.'

'In that case of course I should not dream of allowing you to try. Is that true? You get dizzy?' He looked as stunned as she must have done a few minutes before when she had found out his profession.

She nodded. 'Don't say it. I know—it's all in the mind—yes, I know. It doesn't make me feel any better.'

'I was not going to say that, Victoria.' She was getting used to it now, the way he said her name. 'My mother also, she is the same. It is something that happens. But if you tried ever to ski—on what you call the "nursery slopes", you might conquer that fear.'

She shuddered. 'No thanks.'

'You prefer to remain scared?'

'I prefer to remain on the ground,' she answered smartly. 'I suppose you're frightened of nothing?'

If there was a tinge of sarcasm in her last words, he apparently didn't notice.

He frowned. 'I cannot think of anything at the moment.' I'll just bet you can't, she thought.

She stood up and removed their empty plates. 'I'll make the coffee,' she told him. 'If you'd like to take one lamp into the drawing room, we'll have it there.'

'As you wish. That would be pleasant. But we will go in together, or how would you manage in the dark?'

'I know my way,' she answered. No wonder he moved as he did. With the grace of a ballet dancer, for all his size. And no wonder he had looked so powerful. He was undoubtedly that too. There was no room for weaklings in his kind of existence. He would have had many women—*no*, she thought—to be interrupted by his words:

'I shall carry one lamp through now and return.' He picked the one from the table and went out, diminishing the light in the kitchen by one half. Something else went also, with him, but it was difficult for her to define. There was a sense of loss, as of a powerful presence leaving. She filled the kettle, and in the dim light, began to prepare the percolator. They would have ground coffee this evening, black because powdered milk was no substitute in real coffee, and with liqueurs. She waited for the water to heat up, and thought about him. One of her friends had had a brief romance with a ski instructor when they had all been on holiday, a crowd of them, in the Dolomites a couple of years ago. It had been quite obvious from the start that the Italian, Carlo—a very handsome man of thirty or so—was a ladies' man.

His friend Mario had pursued Victoria relentlessly but she hadn't been interested, and had watched from the sidelines as it were as Ginnie and Carlo had had their brief passionate fling. Ginnie knew what she was doing. A holiday romance was purely and simply that to her, no strings attached. But to Victoria, that didn't appeal. Everyone knew about ski instructors—she shivered at the memories. Ginnie had had to leave a few days before Victoria and the rest of the crowd, and the evening she had left, Carlo had appeared with another blonde on his arm, had winked at Victoria across a crowded room as if to say: 'So what?' She bit her lip. And Gregor had kissed her . . . kissed her. That was all. No more. And had assured her she was safe with him. How safe was safe? Victoria was no prude, but she had had her fingers burned with Peter. She was not going to be burned again in a hurry. It was as well she had discovered what she had about Gregor, because her own thoughts had been taking an alarming turn. She felt herself redden and was thankful he wasn't in the room— then he walked in, soft footed as always, and she took a deep breath.

'Nearly ready,' she said, and poured the boiling water into the percolator. 'What kind of liqueur would you like?'

'Ah. A pleasant thought.' He began to get cups and saucers from a top cupboard 'Benedictine, or Cointreau, if there is any.'

'I'll go and see while you're getting those. They are kept in the dining room.' She switched on the torch, it worked perfectly, and went out, along through the hall to the dining room. It was grimly cold in there and she shivered as she opened the sideboard and shone the light in to find the bottle of Benedictine at the front. She carried it straight into the drawing room together with two glasses then returned to the kitchen.

The coffee had percolated. Together they went to the drawing room, he carrying the lamp and percolator, she with cups, saucers and sugar bowl on a tray. It was all very civilised, and that was how it was going to be now. Until he went off to Aviemore and she remained with her uncle. And she would most probably never see Gregor again. He knelt down to replenish the fire, poking it first, clearing the ash, then placing carefully four logs atop the glowing wood. It was very pleasant in here, like this, he one side of the fireplace, she at the other, the table with coffee and Benedictine between them. How very pleasant it is to be sure, she thought, as she poured two black coffees, then the Benedictine. And I shall ask him about his skiing adventures, and he will tell me, and the conversation will be kept on a light level, and then in a few hours, it will be time for bed, and a good night's sleep before work tomorrow ... I must concentrate, I must——

'What is the matter?' his voice cut into her thoughts and she looked at him surprised.

'What do you mean?'

'I mean what is the matter with you?' he enlarged. 'You are very tense.'

'Me? Tense! Don't be ridiculous!' she retorted. What on earth did he mean? She was totally relaxed. Tense? Why should she be tense?

'Is it because we are here alone?'

'We were alone here last night,' she answered. 'There's no difference.'

'There was no snow last night, and you planned to leave today. There was also power—electricity—I think there is a lot of difference, Victoria.'

He was too shrewd, that was his trouble. Too damned shrewd by far. She looked at him, across the gulf that separated them, a table's breadth but it might have been a world. How could she hope to fool anyone like him when she couldn't even fool herself? And she couldn't speak, could not tell him, for how could she when she didn't know herself? No one had ever spoken to her like that before, probing so deeply and incisively with a few simple words, cutting right through to her inner core of awareness. She didn't like it, and she didn't like him, for if he could see that, what else could he also see? She picked up her coffee cup. Holding it helped.

'So—maybe there is,' she conceded. 'It doesn't mean I'm getting into a panic about the situation. I just—I just—oh! I don't *know*. Leave me alone!' The cup trembled and she put it down lest she drop it. He said nothing, merely looked across the table at her. Then he picked up the glass with the liqueur in it and took a sip.

And all around them, outside, was darkness. And in that large room, just the one area where light shone; the orange bright of a fire, the softer gold of the lamps. Behind them, stretching far back into the room, shadows. There was an intimacy in that. She had made a mistake in suggesting they bring their coffee here. Better in the kitchen—far less personal there. This was a place for lovers to sit, to whisper words for their ears alone, to share laughter. He knew. He knew everything. He watched her, and Victoria did not know, could not know, the picture she made sitting there clad in old jeans and sweater. Was unaware that the soft light enhanced the Madonna-like beauty of her features, and turned her hair to gold that shimmered as she moved. And he could not take his eyes from her. She knew only that those strange and wonderful eyes of his never left her, and she felt helpless under the scrutiny. Her inner distress was transmuted by the gentle glow of lamps into a fine-spun fragility. She picked up her glass and sipped the liquid which tasted fiery after the coffee she had just drunk, and wondered how soon she could escape, and sensed strange emotions swirling round her, her sensitivity heightened to a new pitch of awareness.

It was Gregor who broke the spell, as if he too could no longer bear that stillness of movement. He rose to his feet abruptly, and she glanced up, more relieved than anything at the release from tension. 'I wish to smoke a cigar,' he said, looking down at her, face shadowed, so that she could not see what was in his eyes. 'Have I your permission?'

'Yes.' Thank God for a question with no hidden implications. 'My uncle keeps his in the dining room on the sideboard——'

'I have my own, thank you.' He turned, then he was gone. The door closed softly after him and all was then silent. She poured more coffee and drank it down quickly as if it might give her strength. What was happening to her? She didn't know, and she was afraid. As soon as decently possible, she would go up to her room, have a bath—there might not be many more if the heat went completely—and go to bed with a book and a drink of hot chocolate. That at least tasted much the same with powdered milk. Why did he look at her so? She wanted not to think about him, but the thoughts were irresistible, crowding into her head with an urgency she could not fight any more. She saw the image of him soaring through the air in a faultless arc, swooping down in a breathtaking sweep to land hundreds of feet below and flash like quicksilver down the mountain side. That had been him, a figure of awesome grace and power and speed, and her heart had been in her mouth for a few devastating minutes. And he walked back into the room as silently as he had departed, and sat down, and she said quickly:

'I'm tired. I think I'll go up and have a bath and an early night.'

'Of course.' He leaned forward and put a spill of paper into the flames, lit the thick black cigar, threw the paper in the fire where it vanished in an instant. The aroma of the cigar drifted across to her and she took a deep breath. 'And I shall work in here for a while. I have much to do.' The books she had seen yesterday were not hidden, merely placed on another table in the corner, she saw them now, shadowy and undefined, but there.

Victoria finished her liqueur and stood up. 'I'll clear these away in the morning,' she told him, indicating the glasses and cups. 'Will you excuse me now?'

He too stood up, and for a heart-stopping moment she thought he was going to touch her, but all he said was: 'Yes, of course. Good night, Victoria.' There was an old world formality in his manner. She wondered why her heart should thud so erratically.

'Goodnight, Gregor.' She picked up one of the

lamps; he moved then, towards the door, and opened it, and waited for her to pass him. 'Thank you,' she said, and for a brief moment met his eyes across the lamp. He neither smiled nor spoke, merely inclined his head, and she walked out, steadily, she was relieved to note, and she heard the door close behind her. It was something that had taken no more than a minute, yet an impression was left, an aftertaste in her mind, and it was strange and in a way wonderful—and, in another way, disturbing. Slowly Victoria walked up the stairs, along the corridor to her room and the silence washed in all around her, and if there were ghosts, then this was the time for them, but she saw nothing, heard nothing, only the beat of her own heart and the echo of his words.

Even after a hot soak, in the huge old bath, sleep did not come easily, and when at last it did, was shallow and restless, full of half-waking dreams and images. Victoria woke after a disturbing one that was gone even as she sat up, and squinted at her clock. Nearly three, and she felt headachy and more exhausted than if she had not slept at all. Donning slippers and robe, belting it securely for the air bit raw, she went to the bathroom, and on returning picked up her hot water bottle from where it lay on the carpet. It was scarcely warm. She shivered. Opening her door, clutching the bottle, she walked out, hand on wall for guidance and went cautiously down the stairs. Gregor's bedroom, she had discovered, was nearly opposite hers. His door had been open when she passed it, but she heard no sound. At the foot of the stairs she turned on impulse, and looked along to the drawing room. A faint thread of light showed under the door. Surely he was not still up! She went silently along towards it. The walk seemed longer in the darkness, but that was only her imagination, she knew. Then, at the door she paused, waited. No sounds. No rustling of paper, no aroma of cigars drifting out. She turned the handle and pushed the door open.

The lamp was dim, and it was difficult to see, but no head turned, no voice spoke. Silently she glided across the carpet—and stopped. Gregor lay fast asleep by the embers of a nearly dead fire, and a book had slipped to the floor, open by his feet. On the table, his papers. Coffee and tray had been removed. Her eyes turned again to him. Sprawled out, long legs touching the hearth, he was deeply asleep, head sideways on a cushion, mouth closed, breathing deep and steady. She watched him, there in privacy when he could not see, when no one would know, and although the light was nearly gone, yet she saw enough, his features relaxed in sleep—and of what did he dream?—hard planes of his face softened, eyes shadowed, deep set eyes that had watched her, not seeing anything now save his own inner pictures. She could not leave him thus, it would have been cruel. She knelt on the buffet by his feet and touched his arm.

'Gregor—Gregor——' she said softly, and he stirred, opened his eyes, and looked blankly, unknowingly, at her. He had been—still was—somewhere very far away. 'You've fallen asleep in the chair,' she said, and bent to pick up the book. It was old and heavy. She placed it on the table with the others and when she turned back to face him, he was sitting up rubbing his face.

'Did I fall asleep here?' he asked in a blurred voice, softened now, almost a whisper.

'Yes. I came down for a bottle and saw the light.'

'A bottle?' he repeated stupidly.

'A hot water bottle. It's very cold upstairs.'

He was moving now, stretching, looking round him in apparent disbelief. He looked somehow— vulnerable—a powerful man woken abruptly from a deep slumber and still not sure where he was. He shook his head as if to clear it, and Victoria stood up. She was too near on that footstool. She didn't want to be too near to him. 'I'm sorry I woke you, but you'd have had a stiff neck by morning, staying like that. I'm going into the kitchen now. Would you like a bottle filling?'

A hesitation, as if he still wasn't sure what she meant, then: 'Please—it might be a good idea.'

'Come through when you're ready.' She went out, leaving him the lamp. In the kitchen she filled the kettle, emptied her bottle, found another one and got out the drinking chocolate and powdered milk—and two beakers. Then she waited. She hadn't long. She was glad of her warm dressing-gown, another garment she kept at Drummell House, of thick blue velvety wool material, as unglamorous as a sack, but as warm as a fur coat.

The door opened, light came in followed by Gregor, now awake. 'I'm making myself some hot chocolate as well,' she said. 'I'll make you one too.'

'Thank you.' He sat at the table. She filled the second bottle, capped it tightly and handed it to him.

'Hold that.' She knew he would be feeling cold

after awakening so suddenly. He held it to his chest and she saw the faintest trace of a smile. I have just given a hot water bottle to an Olympic Gold Medallist, she thought, a crazy idiotic thought to have, and that made her smile too, for a different reason. 'Go up to bed,' she said. 'I'll bring your chocolate up. You'll know why I've given you that bottle when you reach your room.' There had been a slight role reversal. It seemed natural for her to be telling him what to do, and she wasn't a bit surprised when he stood up. 'Take the lamp,' she told him. 'I can manage perfectly well.'

'Yes?' He seemed disinclined to demur, and she saw him shiver, and thought, he *is* human after all.

'Yes,' she repeated. She began to mix the drinks, and he picked up the lamp and went out. He won't remember a thing in the morning, she thought, and I won't tell him. The kettle needed filling again, and while she waited for it to boil she clutched the hot water bottle gratefully. The best invention ever, she decided, especially for draughty Scottish houses in winter. They should be made compulsory. She felt remarkably clear headed and wide awake. She felt like singing, which was ridiculous!

Now came the difficult part. She switched off the gas after mixing the drinks, looped her forefinger through both handles—tricky that—and tucked the bottle under the same arm, leaving her left hand free for guidance. Then, steadily and slowly, she went out, along the passage, across the hall, and up the stairs. She tapped on his door and went in to see him lying—still, it seemed—fully dressed, in his bed. He was nearly asleep again. He was no threat to her at all, though why she should think that, she didn't know. She put both beakers down on his bedside table and handed him one. 'Drink that and then you'll sleep,' she said, although it looked as if he would manage perfectly well without any help from hot chocolate or anything else.

'Thank you, Victoria.' He sipped the drink. 'That is good. Very good.' His accent was very pronounced. She stood up, and picked up her own drink.

'Goodnight. Sleep well,' she said.

'Goodnight.' She went out and closed the door softly behind her, and smiled a little smile to herself. Then she scrambled back into her own bed, hot water bottle on her stomach, and sipped her drink. Mmm, it was delicious! A few minutes later she was soundly and deeply asleep.

She was not surprised to find, when she went downstairs the following morning, that Gregor was not up. The house had that chill that spoke of emptiness, and all was silent. She had work to do, if only to prove to herself that she could have managed alone. First the fires to be lit in hall and library and drawing room. By the time she had raked the ashes and put them outside she was smudged and dirty, but she was full of energy, and soon had the three fires burning satisfactorily. She washed the previous night's dishes, found peas and beans in the freezer—kept carefully closed to preserve the cold as long as possible—and left them in the kitchen to thaw, smiling as she did so. Thaw! They might freeze again if she put them in her bedroom instead. The kitchen was warming up for she had put the Aga oven on, and it had sufficient power to heat the entire room. Outside the snow sparkled pure and clear in a watery sun, and it shone in through the window palely. But it *was* daylight, no need for lamps now, and her mood was as light. How foolish she had been the previous night!

She cleaned the kitchen surfaces so that all shone and welcomed. If only she had. some flowers! And then she remembered. There were some—even if they would be buried under the snow, she knew exactly where they were, and the snow would have preserved them. It took her only minutes to don wellingtons and mac, find a shovel and scissors and set off for the front door. A blast of icy air hit her as she opened it and she caught her breath. 'Ouch!' she said.

Past his car, struggling through, wishing she hadn't bothered, but determined now, she reached the rose beds at last, and was perspiring freely, felt around—hands like two frozen lumps, would *they* ever thaw out?—gently now, nearly there—ah! That was it!

Bending, scissors ready she scooped the snow gently away from the late-blooming roses and snipped the stems. Three was enough—it would have to be enough or her hands would drop off— and carried them back triumphantly. They were slightly battered but intact. She found a small vase, filled it with water and placed the roses in with loving care, setting it on the table. Then she stood back to look at them, giving a deep sigh of satisfaction.

And Gregor walked in, soft footed, looking as though he had slept in his clothes, confirming her suspicions, looking also dark and unshaven. He carried his hot water bottle and empty beaker. She turned to him. 'Good morning, did you sleep well?'

'Good morning. Yes——' he hesitated. 'Did I go to sleep down here?' He had forgotten—or nearly anyway.

'Yes, you did. I came down at three and found you.'

He looked at the bottle he held. 'I woke up with that.' He sounded puzzled.

'Well you would. I gave it to you.' She could meet his eyes very well now. Her mood of confidence would not easily be displaced. She felt splendid. The fact that he looked as though he was suffering from a severe hangover had nothing to do with it she was sure. 'Shall I make you a cup of coffee or tea?'

'Tea please, no milk.' He sat down at the table and stifled a yawn. Then he saw the flowers—and looked up at her.

She smiled. 'I thought a few roses would be nice so I went and picked these.'

'In the snow?'

'Yes.' The kettle had been bubbling for some moments. She made the tea, put two beakers on the table and mixed a pint of milk in the jug, from the powder. 'I can make you toast—not alas in the toaster, but by the hall fire.'

'No. I am not hungry.' He added, belatedly, 'Thank you.' He rubbed his neck. 'May I have a bath?'

'Of course. There should be hot water.' She poured the tea out for both of them and sat down. Gregor looked at her for the first time.

'I must apologise for putting you to any trouble.'

'It was no trouble. I came down to fill a hot water bottle, and found you fast asleep by the fire.'

'I worked until about two o'clock, I remember that, for I heard a clock chime in the distance. And then——' he shrugged, 'I do not remember anything else until I seemed to be drinking chocolate in bed.' He frowned. 'And I held that.' He pointed towards the fat rubber bottle—'and was not sure how it had arrived. But ah, it was so warm. I did not realise.'

She laughed. 'Don't tell me they don't have them where you live! They must do.'

'Of course. But they are for old people and children——' he stopped. It was clear he realised what he had just said.

'And,' Victoria cut in rapier swift, 'for winters in snowbound Scottish houses.'

A smile twitched at the corner of his mouth. 'Yes, that too,' he admitted.

'So you might have one tonight?' she queried.

'I think that I might,' he conceded gravely.

'You said you would make bread today,' she reminded him. 'All we have are a few slices of rather stale bread. Fine for toast, but——' she shrugged.

'Yes I will do so, of course. There is strong flour and yeast powder, that too is something I noticed yesterday.'

'Have you made it before? It's not easy you know.'

'You have tried?'

'Once,' she said in dry tones. 'During a bread strike. If I remember right, even the birds turned up their noses at it!'

'Then I shall show you. It is easy when it is explained.'

Why not? There was no terrible urgency. Snow had that effect. It was almost as if time slowed, became less important. She had already tasted his cooking, which was in a class of its own, and there was something very primitive about the ritual of making bread—and there was also the strangest sensation in his nearness, but that awareness was buried deeply, she was not even conscious of it. She only knew that it seemed to be the only thing she could have ever wanted to do that very morning. 'Thank you. I would like to watch.'

'And while it is preparing itself by the fire——' he had a quaint way of expressing himself sometimes, no doubt about it, 'I will go and see if there is anything I can do to repair the ladder, to make it stronger, you understand.'

'You might be able to strengthen the ladder. It won't make any difference to my stupid fear,' she said wryly.

'But I will be there.'

'So?' She wanted to say—but didn't. The unconscious arrogance of his words implied that *that* would make it all right. And perhaps it would. 'Yes. You'll be there,' she answered instead.

He drank his tea in two long swallows and stood up. 'Then I shall go and bathe now.' He put his cup in the sink and walked out. She watched him go. She had never met a man quite like him. So tremendously self-assured—and yet, and yet, she had seen him at his most vulnerable, freshly awakened in unfamiliar surroundings; and there had been a difference then, oh such a difference. She had glimpsed, for a few minutes, another, gentler man. She knew why she had got up from the footstool so quickly. For a brief moment she had had the urge to take him in her arms, to hold him to her like a child and comfort him—and that was the most ridiculous idea to have! For a second though, her fingers had tingled to touch his face, to stroke and smooth—and reassure.

'I must be mad,' she said out loud, and that was better. It brought normality back. She washed the beakers under the cold tap. 'Quite crazy, Victoria Mitchell. What are you? You're an idiot, that's what you are.' And she laughed for such foolishness. But she was rather glad that there was no one to hear her, for they might wonder why she spoke thus to herself, and she didn't really know.

CHAPTER FIVE

IT was very satisfying, perched up on a kitchen stool, feet hooked on a rung, hot coffee cup in hands, watching someone else work, Victoria decided. Operation Bread was in progress. And Gregor wasn't doing it by halves. He was making sufficient dough to last for *weeks*. The extra would be wrapped in foil and buried in deep snow where it would keep fresh until needed. When the snow vanished and electricity was restored, then it could be placed in the freezer. His explanation, and his method of working, was quite fascinating. He would probably have made a good teacher, she thought.

It was mid morning, and the kitchen was covered in a fine mist of flour. So much for her cleaning efforts before! She was not allowed to do anything, save measure off lengths of foil, and this she had done. Gregor had returned after his bath, changed into different clothes—and she had had to hide that first shock upon seeing him return. No longer the fisherman's jersey and jeans, but a pair of tight fitting black corduroys and a black cashmere sweater that had, for a moment, made her heart contract in mingled pain and surprise. The pain—for he could not know but it made it no less agonising—was because Peter had similar clothes, and had worn them on their one visit together here. And if Gregor had worn that outfit on his arrival it was no wonder Uncle Craig had mistaken the man. The surprise—because in them he looked superb, there was no other word for it. Superb. She could almost visualise him skiing down a mountain dressed thus in black, a heart-stopping image of sheer power and male beauty. Oh yes, this was a man of great force, and power—and overwhelming sexuality. He exuded such an air of intense virility that it was difficult to look normally at him. And he was *unaware of it*. Of that Victoria was certain. She had met many men. The blatant sexual awareness of some was off-putting to say the least. The 'look at me, aren't I *something*?' so unmistakable, so *obvious*. But in Gregor, nothing like that. No glances, awaiting the spark of admiration. Nothing. And in a strange way, it made him a more powerful force.

It was relief almost leading to laughter when he had donned Mrs Holt's plainest apron—it only had 'Scotland for Ever' and a picture of a thistle emblazoned on it. Her taste in aprons was weird and wonderful, and Victoria usually managed to find a new one to bring her each time she visited—and this was one of the less flamboyant ones, but it covered him effectively and that was what mattered. And now, an hour later, she watched as he wrapped the unraised dough in foil before kneading the raised dough that would make the next two days' supply of fresh bread, and she sighed a little unheard sigh as she watched.

I am here, she thought, watching a champion skier demonstrate how to make bread, and there is no one I can tell about it. There was something rare and precious about, some atmosphere that defied description. It was happening all the time, a growing sense of awareness—and she knew, with a deep feminine instinct, that *he* was as aware of it as her. She *knew*. It was like—almost like—difficult even to muster her thoughts—like a kind of fine golden mist surrounding them. Very odd to even be thinking those thoughts but they were there all the same. And sometimes, when he looked at her, when she met his eyes, she saw what was in his and her heart quickened. Oh yes, whatever this thing was, he knew too. Yet it could not be spoken, for how could it? She wanted him to touch her. No, no, that was stupid, wasn't it? Of course she didn't. She shifted on her stool and dismissed such stupidity. Of course she *didn't*.

She had to clear her throat before she could speak. 'Shall I fetch in the bread from the hall?' she asked.

'No. It is too heavy for you.' He was finished now, the last foil-wrapped parcel on the table. 'But we will take these out now, to the front of the house, near my car.'

'Why the front?'

He looked at her. 'Because that is north—and colder.' It seemed an elementary lesson, and she had forgotten, so how should he know? She felt herself go pink. Of course. She slid off the stool.

'Right,' she said. Loaded with shiny, crackly lumps of silver dough they made their way through the hall, and he opened the door. There, just outside, the bread was deposited with due ceremony and covered in tight-packed snow. He worked quickly. The air was bitter chill, and their breath turned to steam as it left their mouths, and the sound of silence from all around was almost deafening. Victoria began to shiver and he said,

'Go in,' and she answered,

'Not until you've done,' and crouched beside him at their improvised freezer. Then, finished and they were in, and closing the door after them. Her hands and ears started to throb with relief from the cold, and her face glowed. And he took her arm before she could move away, and it startled her until he spoke. 'Wait,' he said. 'Wait, Victoria.' And he looked down at her.

'W-what is it?'

'What time is it now?'

'Nearly eleven-fifteen—why?'

'And what time do you have news bulletins on the radio?'

'Twelve—but we haven't got any——' her voice faltered into silence as she followed the direction of his pointing hand, through the narrow window at the side of the door. 'Of *course*,' she whispered. 'Your *car*! You have a *radio*!'

'Yes.'

'But—will it still work—the battery——'

'I hope so. We will see. At twelve—or just before of course, we will put our coats on and go and see shall we?'

It would be interesting to have a link, however brief, with the world. She nodded. 'Oh yes.' And why hadn't it occurred to her?

'Then let us go and make a warm drink. We have time,' he had released her, was crossing to the hearth, to the cloth-covered mixing bowl, lifting the cloth, prodding gently, 'we will put the bread in the oven first, and it will be baking.' He lifted the bowl. He was right, it was heavy, it was huge and full, enough there for four loaves, never mind two. Infinite possibilities—fresh crusty buttered bread, garlic bread, cinnamon toast—her mouth watered. They could live on those, if they had to, if all else failed. Bread, and melted snow boiled in a kettle on an open fire. They could live like royalty. There was something special about him ... something extraordinary. ...

Hot coffee again, hands growing less red, face ceasing to tingle, ears not hurting, Victoria sat and watched as the kneaded dough was cut and shaped—all sorts of shapes—everything had been brought into play; a cake tin, a baking dish, flan dishes. There would be square bread, and rolls, and a long narrow loaf done in a paté tin, and even, with some left over, a cottage loaf.

He washed his hands, dusted the flour from him as she cleaned the table top and he drank his coffee, and it was five to twelve. Victoria fetched the macs and wellingtons, and they set off again to the hall. He had covered all windows on his car with newspaper, as well as the radiator, and when she slid in, it was eerily dark inside. Two minutes to go. Gregor closed his door and turned the ignition key and switched on the radio. A burst of static, snatches of music, then he turned to her. 'You had better find the station,' he said. 'I do not know your British radio.'

'Of course.' Radio Two, she twiddled the dial, found it, heard the closing music of Jimmy Young. They were just in time. Nearness, strong awareness of that nearness, a closed, intimate atmosphere. He by her side inches away, listening as intensely as her. No scent of aftershave on him, yet he was freshly shaven, no perfume at all, yet an awareness stronger than any scent beat her heart swifter. It was cold, so cold, she shivered, and he put his arm round her as she had known he would do, and

held her. Then—'Shh,' she whispered, and the
news came on. They listened, or perhaps he
listened. She tried, but the words weren't making
sense. Trouble in the Middle East, a cease fire
broken, three people rescued from a fire in
Woking—the weather causing increasing concern,
especially in Eastern regions and particularly in
North East Scotland where power failures were
adding to the chaos, all roads blocked—on and on
it went, no sign of a thaw. Helicopters flying over
remote regions, food being airlifted to farms. . . . It
was over, and he switched off, turned the key,
removed it. Then he looked at her. 'We may be
here longer than we think,' he said. He was too
close, much too close.

'Yes. So it seems,' she agreed. Her parents
wouldn't be worried. They knew she was capable—
and they knew she was with Ivan Shenkov's son.
But they didn't know *him*. They didn't know
anything about him or the effect he was having on
their daughter. And Uncle Craig would be nearly
ready to come home, and impatient to be there,
but with no way of doing so. They were as cut off
from the world as if they were on a remote island.

'Come, we must go in again,' he said, and she
followed him out, and they ran the few yards to
the door, and then were inside. They took off their
wellingtons and macs and he said: 'We will leave
them here. Later, again, we will listen. Once or
twice a day. Then we will know what is
happening.'

'Yes,' she went to the fire, held her hands out,
and he came up behind her, stood closely behind
her, put his arms round her and hugged her like he
would a small child who needed comforting.

'It is all right, Victoria,' his voice soft in her ear.

'I—know.' He had sensed her innermost despair, had picked it up as if by telepathy. Her back was warm with his body. She didn't want him to move away. Perhaps he considered her as a child, someone to be protected. Her whole body tingled in the awareness of him. He wasn't as clever as she thought if he didn't know that. But perhaps he did, for the next moment he moved abruptly away.

'And now,' he said, his voice slightly different. 'You will prepare lunch while I see that ladder. Something simple today I think. Eggs on toast yes?'

'Very easy. Yes. Then I'll look out those books for you.' The ladder was essential. The ceilings were very high. Two chairs on top of each other— even if that were feasible—would not reach the highest two shelves. The sooner he got his books down, the sooner they would be able to work separately. She went towards the kitchen, leaving him in the hall. She didn't look back. She wanted to, but she didn't.

'It is old. There is not much anyone can do.' They were standing in the library, and Victoria looked up at the ladder in some dismay. It was on runners that attached to the highest row, and had tiny wheels at the base. It slid along easily, and it was terribly *high*—and very rickety. It looked, to her eyes, as fragile as though it were made of glass, not wood.

'No. I can see that,' she agreed. She took a deep breath. 'Well, here goes.' If he could leap off a mountain top and into space at something over a

hundred miles an hour, then she could climb a
ladder. One thing was certain. She was going to *do*
it. And *now*. She put her foot on the bottom step,
and went slowly up. He held the base as steady as
a rock. That was something. She reached the top.
Thank God for that handle sticking up. She
searched the shelf in front of her and resolutely did
not look down, even though her heart hammered
and her head was going to burst. This was
ridiculous! She saw the carefully handwritten
words on the spines of half a dozen books. These
then were what her uncle had been looking for
when he tumbled down. The ladder creaked under
her. With her free hand—the other grasping the
upright handle so tightly it might need prising
off—she began to ease the first book out, bent her
knees as far as she was able, not looking down at
him, said: 'Can you reach that?'

'Yes.' It was taken from her. Then the next, and
the next, then all done. Time to come down. A
large gap yawned on the shelf. It had been easy, of
course it had. *He* was there. Backwards, slowly,
nearly down—and she was being lifted, plucked
off the ladder, as though featherlight, and placed
safely on the floor. He wasn't laughing. It was
hard to tell his expression but his voice held
laughter, just a trace of it, as he said:

'Clever girl.'

'Aren't I just?' She looked up, then, at him. The
books were on the floor beside them. 'I dare say
there are more. I can do it again.'

'But not alone. Only with me here.' He was
quite serious.

'Believe me, I wouldn't try.' It was true—he *did*
think of her as a child who needed telling what to

do. And why fight that? Victòria, an independent,
modern-minded girl, who was perfectly well used
to looking after herself, found the thought
intriguing. He would take charge—he already had
in a way, and she would let him. No man she had
ever known had ever bossed her, or even tried to.
It was a new sensation—and that he was capable
was in no doubt. He thought ahead, planned,
organised—except once, so recently, when it was
she who had taken command, and he had been
more than half asleep. And she would not forget
that, not for a long time, until he was long gone
out of her life. . . . She was suddenly cold, and
turned away.

Now was time to get back to work. All the fires
burned brightly, had been replenished after lunch,
and Gregor was working in the drawing room. He
had been writing, she had seen a stack of papers
spread out on his working table when she had
gone in after lunch with a basket of logs while he
did hall and library, and she had paused on her
way to the fire, and looked. He wrote in French,
not Russian, black upright writing that could only
belong to a man like him, sheets and sheets of
details and dates set neatly out.

She wondered how much he had discovered,
how far he had traced back. There was something
fascinating about the thought that somewhere in
his history there might have been the same Scots
blood as ran in her veins. It would be, in a way, a
link.

She worked well in the library until the light
grew less and it was difficult to see fine print any
more, stretched herself, and went to make coffee.
The kitchen was warm, filled with that delicious

aroma of freshly baked bread. She picked up the cottage loaf and sniffed it. Ah, delicious. The crust was firm and crackled faintly as she put it back. He could make bread too. She wondered vaguely if there was anything he couldn't do.

She filled two beakers and went in to see him sitting engrossed, writing. For a moment she hesitated to disturb him. It was clear he had not heard her come in. But surely he couldn't see sufficiently well now? The room was almost grey. Even though he had moved his table nearer the window, what light was coming in was negligible. It would be time to light the lamps any minute now. She walked silently across to stand behind him. Still no reaction, instead a concentration that excluded everything. She put the beakers down in the hearth and sat. His voice came: 'I will be one minute, Victoria.'

'It's all right. It's only coffee.'

He didn't answer her. There had been something, a suppressed excitement in his words. She could see him continuing to write in pitch darkness, on and on. He was copying from a book open in front of him—translating as he went on, obviously. No wonder he hadn't heard her come in. He was silhouetted against the window, dark, broad-shouldered outline, head bent, black hair, blacker still with night. The man from the past. . . .

'Ah! It is done. For now.' He turned. She had not imagined his excitement, it was there in his face—what she could see of his face anyway, a grey blur, no more. He looked round then. 'It is nearly dark!' he announced in surprise, as if she might not be aware of the fact.

Her tone was dry. 'I *know*. What I don't

understand is how you could see to write anything.'

He turned and glanced at the papers he had just been writing on. 'Nor do I, now,' he answered.

'What is it? Have you found something of interest? You were totally engrossed when I came in just now.'

'Yes. I was. And—yes—I have found many interesting things.' He lit the lamp that had been left on the mantelpiece and threw a log on the fire and the room became different again. It was home. It had always been home—as inextricably a part of her as her family. She had thought that Gregor had changed things, but he hadn't. She left a part of her heart here whenever she went away, and when she returned, was complete. Her grandparents had lived here, and her great-grandparents before them, and so on, back for several generations.

Uncle Craig, whose wife had died some twenty years previously, without children, would not be able to continue the line, and there was a sadness, a sense of loss in that knowledge. Neither Victoria's brother or sister, much as they enjoyed visits, had ever felt the sense of total belonging that she did. Uncle Craig knew though, and to him, Victoria was in a sense the daughter he had never had. She loved him as much as she loved her parents. It had never needed to be said, never would be, it was simply *there*, that knowledge they both shared. She felt very close to him at that moment, and wondered what he was doing in hospital. Reading no doubt. If there were only a dozen books in the entire hospital, he would have found them. She smiled at the thought. And waited. Gregor was looking through his papers by the light from the lamp, absorbed again, checking something, face intent. He looked at her suddenly, as if aware she had been watching him.

'Forgive me, I am very rude,' he said. 'But I need to——' even as he spoke, his eyes returned to the papers. Whatever he had discovered—or thought he had—was clearly of such importance that he needed time to think. Victoria, who had been sipping her coffee quietly while she waited, and thought too of her own matters, rose to her feet.

'No you're not. I did interrupt you, I can see that. Look—I'll go into the kitchen and find something for us to eat while you carry on here. Just don't forget to drink your coffee, all right?'

He was relieved, she could tell. 'If that is no trouble——'

'I wouldn't have offered if it was.' She was curious, certainly intrigued, but she would get no sense out of him at the moment. Clearly whatever he had found needed thinking over. There was plenty to do in the kitchen, and old newspapers to do the crosswords in before they were used to light the fires. She would wait there until *he* came out. It was quite cosy in the kitchen sitting with feet up by the Aga. And she might even help herself to a glass of sherry. 'I'll see you there when you're ready.'

His eyes were on the papers again. She sensed the effort it was to drag them away and look at her. 'Yes. Thank you.'

She walked away. At the door, she turned. He had put the lamp on the table, and his head was bent. He had probably forgotten her existence. With a little shrug, she went out.

She put the lamp on the table at the end nearest the Aga, placed a thick cushion on the ancient wooden rocking chair that sat in the far corner of the kitchen and dragged it to the warmth, opened the first newspaper, a three-month-old *Observer*, found the section with the crossword in, and began to do it. The bottle of sherry, and two glasses—in the remote possibility that he might arrive within the next hour or two—were on the table as well. Victoria poured herself a generous glassful and sipped it as she considered one across, pen poised ready for action.

She liked sherry, and was rather surprised to find, when she picked up the glass for a thoughtful sip as she wrestled with ten down, that it was empty. She poured herself another. It was difficult to concentrate on the crossword with the questions buzzing in her head, but she tried. And how on earth had those books come to be here—and *how* had *he* known they would be? No. The crossword. He would tell her soon, until then it was no use speculating. Just wait. It was extremely pleasant, just sitting here, rocking gently from time to time, feet up on a chair, sherry glass to hand, damned crossword proving increasingly difficult. 'Try another, Victoria,' she said out loud. 'No, that's cowardly.' She giggled. That's the second time I've talked to myself, she thought, and what the hell—there's only him to hear and he won't appear for ages. He'll probably fall asleep again in that chair—did I come out here for something? Apart from crosswords and sherry—terribly civilised my dear—she giggled again. Oh yes, dinner. Food. That stuff you eat from time to time. Well, it could wait. She picked up the bottle, frowned at it,

poured some into the glass and squinted down at
the crossword. Gracious, that lamp was getting
dimmer. She was *sure* the print hadn't been
blurrèd before. She took a thoughtful swallow of
sherry while she considered the matter. Perhaps
her eyes were tired. Yes, that was it. Come to think
of it, *she* was feeling rather tired as well. No not
exactly *tired*, but—she frowned. A bit—confused.
She threw the paper to one side, leaned to pick up
another one, and missed. The kitchen swayed,
gently, quite gently, but a definite swaying
movement. Victoria stared accusingly at the bottle.
That was it! It was powerful stuff that. Very nice
though. A *little* drop more wouldn't hurt—would
it? No. Of course not. And when he came out, he'd
join her. Might even make the breakfast. No. She
frowned. That wasn't right. Not breakfast. Dinner.
Yes.

She closed her eyes, just for a second, and when
she opened them a few minutes later she wasn't
sure where she was. Her head ached. She stood up
and had to hold the table. 'Oh.' She groaned.

She would go and find Gregor and ask him to
help her with dinner—or whatever meal it was she
had to do. Where was the damned torch? Oh, yes
there it was. She switched it on and walked out of
the kitchen, along the passage and into the hall.
Across that, *very steadily* and *carefully*—where
was he?

'Gregor,' she shouted, standing at the end of the
corridor. *'Gregor!'* She, Victoria Mitchell, was not
going looking for him. The door at the far end
opened. For a moment this large dark shape stood
silhouetted in the doorway and it was so like that
other time—so like some other time, aeons ago—

someone *from* another time—then he was moving, coming towards her, walking quickly, saying something but she couldn't hear, her head was going round and the carpet was coming up to meet her.

'Gregor—I——' she began, and felt him catch her just before the carpet reached her. Oh, that was a relief. . . .

'What have you been drinking?' His voice wasn't kind. It was harsh, and hard, and she didn't like it one bit. Victoria found she was lying on the long pink settee near the fire in the drawing room. Her head throbbed relentlessly and she put her hand to it. What did he mean?

'What?' she whispered.

Gregor sat down beside her, and she stared at him. 'You are drunk,' he said.

'Drunk? Don't be silly! I only had a glass of sherry——'

'How many glasses?'

'Well—two—maybe three. *I* don't know!' she shouted. 'What right have *you* to——'

'When you collapse at my feet, Victoria, I have the right. We are alone here. I cannot get you to a doctor if you are ill, remember? Or have you forgotten we are snowbound?'

'I haven't forgotten that you are bloody rude!' she retorted. He pulled her to her feet, roughly, not gently at all.

'Come with me.'

'No I damned well won't——' she lashed out at him and missed. The next moment he picked her up, grabbed the torch, and carried her out of the room. 'Put me down!' she gasped, astounded beyond belief at his action. He didn't reply. The torch beam bobbed in front of them along the corridor, all the way back to the kitchen where he dumped her unceremoniously in a chair and picked up the sherry bottle. He held it in front of her face.

'Show me how full the bottle was,' he demanded. She stared angrily at him, then sensing he would keep on asking if she didn't reply, said:

'It was full.'

'I see.' He went very calm, quite suddenly. Then he came over to her again and lifted her to her feet. Carefully, not roughly as he had before. 'Come to the sink.' She allowed him to lead her, all resistance gone. She wanted to cry. 'I am going to give you something to drink that will make you sick. Then perhaps you will feel better.'

'No!' she gasped.

'*Yes.*' The voice was steel.

He poured water into a beaker, added a generous measure of salt, stirred it and handed it to her. 'Drink.' A pause. 'If you do not, I will make you drink it, and believe me, you will not like that.' His tone was deadly. She shivered. He meant it, every word. She was feeling too ill to care. She pinched her nose and drank it down in one long swallow. He went away and returned with a towel.

'Now, put your finger at the back of your throat——' he began, but his instruction was unnecessary. Moments later a white-faced Victoria stumbled to the table and sat down. She felt wretched, but her head was clearing rapidly. She put her head on the cool table and closed her eyes. She heard the taps being run, then the kettle being filled, and her heart was thudding as though it might burst.

'Sit up.' His voice was gentle, not like before. She obeyed, and Gregor bent over her and sponged her face with a warm flannel. 'Do you feel better?' he asked.

She nodded. 'A little. I'm—sorry.'

'You had drunk a third of a bottle. On an empty stomach it could have been very dangerous.'

'I didn't—know——'

'You were foolish. I am filling for you a hot water bottle. You will go to bed now, and I will bring some toast up for you, and a drink of tea with no milk. That is all. You understand?'

'Yes.'

He handed her the bottle. 'Do you wish me to come up with you?'

She wanted to say no, to let him see that she was fine, but she could not. 'Please,' she whispered.

He led her up the stairs and to her room, leaving the torch alight on the table, enough for her to see by. 'Clean your teeth and wash your face. Keep your clothes on if that is warmer. I shall return in ten minutes.' She sat on the bed.

'Thank you.' He melted away like a shadow. Taking a deep breath, Victoria got up and went to the bathroom, holding the torch. When he came back, she was in bed, clutching the hot bottle, and shivering. He carried a tray with a lamp, beaker, and plate on, put them down on the floor and sat on the bed.

'How are you now?' he asked.

'Better—sober—and sorry,' she answered in a small voice. 'Gregor—I——'

'No. Nothing is necessary. Take this.' He gave

her the beaker. 'Sip slowly.' The tea was strong, slightly sweetened, with no milk. She obediently sipped it and he handed her the plate with a slice of dry toast on. She pulled a face. 'Ugh. Do I have to——'

'Yes.' She chewed a piece and sipped her tea. Then another piece, another sip. He watched her steadily. She was beginning to be capable of coherent thought now. She had eaten so little at lunch, and nothing at breakfast. She was extremely hungry. No wonder the sherry had had such a devastating effect! She would never touch it again as long as she lived. But she couldn't try and explain, because he would not let her. He knew, anyway. He knew everything.

'What time is it?' she asked, when the toast was gone.

'Nearly seven. What time is the news?'

She frowned. 'I'm not sure. Probably at seven——'

'I will go and try. You are to rest here.'

'But——'

He stood up, taking empty plate and beaker from her. 'Yes. For now. I will leave you the lamp.' He picked up the torch. 'I will return in half an hour.' And he was gone. She looked at the lamp, then snuggled down into bed. He had told her to keep her clothes on, and she had, even her socks. She was getting warmer now, quite cosy in fact. She closed her eyes, and drifted away, far away. . . .

Light bloomed, a voice spoke her name softly: 'Victoria——' and she opened her eyes to see Gregor standing there bathed in light, the shadows behind him and for a moment she thought she was still dreaming. Then he spoke again, and it was no dream. 'It is nearly ten o'clock.'

'Have I been asleep?' She sat up. Apart from a dull headache she felt fine.

'Yes. You are better now?'

'Yes.'

'Good. So—would you like to come down and eat?'

'Yes.' She didn't ask what. She was *starving*.

'I will see you downstairs, when you are ready.' And he was gone. Victoria carried the lamp he had left into the bathroom and washed herself, then went downstairs. It was obvious that he had already eaten, and she wondered what. For her there was simple fare, a plate of vegetables, no trimmings, no meat. Sensible, she knew, and it served her right, and she was not disposed to argue. Gregor read one of the old newspapers while she ate, and when she had finished, he said: 'Do you feel fit enough to look for any more books?'

'Tonight?'

'Yes.'

He wanted her to climb that ladder again? Was that why he had woken her—cooked her a meal? Was something so important that it could not wait until morning? She took a deep breath. He had done a lot for her, and she owed him for that. 'Yes, of course I will,' she answered.

'Good.'

'Can you tell me why?' she asked.

'There are several books still that I need. I have searched all the library shelves except of course those I cannot reach. I dare not take the chance on climbing the ladder—not as things are you understand——'

'No.' She understood that, and shuddered. 'And this—search—is very important to you, isn't it?'

'Yes.' A simple answer to a simple question. He had made tea. She drank hers while she thought about that. He had an inexorable quality to him, a single mindedness she had already seen, the total absorption in what he was doing. But he had already been there several days with her uncle. Had he not already seen all he wanted?

'Why are you so sure there are more books? Would Uncle Craig not have known what you wanted?'

'No, for I did not exactly know myself, Victoria. It is a complicated story. It goes back a long time, to when my father, and your uncle, first met in Paris over twenty years ago. My father too has a great love of books—they were introduced to each other at the apartment of a mutual friend who had a bookshop then in the centre of Paris. Your uncle was an old customer of Leon's——' Victoria remembered the name vaguely, Uncle Craig was probably on first name terms with owners of bookshops all over Europe '—and he and my father found a lot in common immediately.' He paused. Intrigued, Victoria waited. 'My father worked in a restaurant then—he had only recently left Russia, after a great deal of difficulty—and lived in a very small apartment with my mother and brother. I was away at *lycée*—school, and never met your uncle, although I was told much about him afterwards. The apartment had originally belonged to an uncle of my father's, who had left Russia before the Revolution. He had lived

there for many years—and there was a box of
books that he had left, containing our family
history, among many other things, a subject which
interested my father very much—which also
interested your uncle, because in this collection of
books were several linking us with this part of
Scotland.' He stopped, and Victoria said:

'This part? You have ancestors who came from
around *here*?'

'Yes.' She remembered then his words, so long
ago, or had it only been two days? 'Some of my
family history is here.' Remembered too, her
surprise at them, the shock on hearing them. With
all that had happened, scarcely surprising she
should have forgotten them. She sighed. 'I can see
why you're so interested. And you found
something very intriguing this afternoon, didn't
you?'

He smiled. 'Oh yes. I found out that in 1825 a
woman called Victoria Mitchell married a Russian
and went back to Russia with him—and she is an
ancestor of mine.'

'Victoria Mitchell?' she whispered, absolutely
stunned. *'Victoria Mitchell?'*

'So. You also find that as fascinating? I can see
from your face——'

'I—I can't believe it——'

'It is true. What I am trying to establish now is
whether she is also a relative of yours. The name
Mitchell is, I know, not uncommon.'

'Nor was the name Victoria. There has always
been a Victoria in practically every generation——'
she paused at the significance of her *own* words,
and she looked at him, and there was that quiet air
of stillness about them, as in the calm before a

storm, the stillness of waiting that precedes something tremendous. It built up to a sharp pitch of awareness. Those eyes of his, watching her, steady, strangely exciting eyes, just watching, waiting, waiting. . . . She could scarce bear it a moment longer.

'What was the name of the man she married?' she asked, mouthing the words, because she already felt as if she knew the answer.

'His name was Gregor. Gregor Shenkov.'

CHAPTER SIX

IT was many hours later, though how late, Victoria had no idea. The books lay scattered on the carpet by the fire and they both sat on footstools. Easier that way—and warmer. The fire burnt brightly, ash thick beneath it. All was silence around them, and Victoria was struggling to keep awake, after a fruitless search of several more dusty tomes. She yawned, and Gregor, seeing, said: 'We must stop now.'

'So many threads—so much,' she murmured, stroking the page of an album of newspaper cuttings, neatly pasted in by a Mitchell long dead and gone. This was living history, the history of her family painstakingly gathered over the years, never before explored by her—nor, she suspected by Uncle Craig himself.

The first shock had worn off, of hearing Gregor's name linked with a woman who could be an ancestor, what remained now was strange, a sensation of wonder, almost, a sense of family brought back to vivid animation and colour. It was like breathing life into those long passed away, seeing how their lives had been, feeling a part of it all. As she was. She was proud of her ancestry. But the call of sleep was greater. She rubbed her arms and looked at Gregor. 'Yes,' she agreed, 'we must stop.' She looked at the fire burning so brightly, and shivered, thinking of the icy cold bedrooms to which they must go now, and Gregor said softly:

'It is cold upstairs.'

'I know.' She no longer felt surprise at his ability to pick her thoughts.

'We can stay here, Victoria.' Again that name, said thus, and now with added piquancy. For was that how his ancestor had pronounced the name of his bride? And had she too heard it, and been as fascinated?

'Here? In this room?'

'It is sensible.'

She looked round her at the darkness behind and all round them. Her bones ached with her utter exhaustion. Yes, it was sensible, but was it wise? She looked at him, and his face was dark and expressionless, waiting for her to speak. 'On chairs?' she asked.

'They would not be very comfortable, I think. No, I have a better idea. It occurred to me an hour or so ago. If we lie together in my sleeping bag we will be warm.'

Was he saying what she thought he was saying? Eyes wide, she glanced across at him, and there was a sudden stillness in the air. She took a deep breath. 'Oh, no,' she began, 'I don't——'

'No.' His voice cut in harshly. 'It is not what *you* think, Victoria——'

'You've just suggested we sleep together in a sleeping bag. What am I supposed to think?'

'That we are in a situation which is not ordinary, that it is essential we keep warm—and that I can provide the means. *That* is what you are supposed to think.' He rose to his feet, towering over her, a large man who might be angry, she could not quite tell. 'However,' he went on, and his voice was cold, 'that is what *I* shall do.' He turned and walked away towards the door leaving Victoria wordless. She began to gather up the scattered books, carry them to the table by the window, aware sharply of the drop in temperature in those few yards. She pulled back the heavy velvet curtain. Bleak whiteness lay outside, harsh and relentless. Winters would have been like this nearly two hundred years ago when another Victoria Mitchell had gone to an unknown new world with the man she loved. And had she too looked out of this very window, and seen the same trees and mountains? Had she, on a clear day, looked out, and stored up the memories to take with her across the thousands of miles? Victoria's heart ached for that unknown girl who had left Scotland behind for ever. . . .

She turned at the opening of the door and Gregor came in with a large, rolled-up bundle. Silently he went over to the fireplace, and Victoria, too cold to remain by the window any longer, returned and stood at the side of the fireplace, and watched. He had brought a mattress down as well. He laid that down first then covered it with the bright orange sleeping bag, which was of thick padded nylon. She held her hands to the fire, the back of her cold, away from it. He straightened up, and looked at her, but didn't speak. And she knew what she must say.

'I'm sorry,' she said. 'I was foolish.'

'Yes, you were. To think I meant anything wrong. You have changed your mind?'

'Yes, if it's not too late.'

'No, it is not too late. I will go and fetch our pillows. Will you fill a hot water bottle? We will only need one.'

'Yes.' She picked up the torch, and went out. She heard him follow her a few moments later, but didn't look back. One bottle, that was all they would need, because they would be sleeping together. Only not in the sense in which that expression was generally understood. Together— but not together. Her heart had quickened its beat. He was being eminently sensible. A born survivor, a man who would know how to cope in any adverse conditions—and she had reacted to his suggestion as though he had proposed seduction! She was too tired to think straight now. She filled the kettle by torchlight, and the kitchen was deathly cold. It would be a relief to get back in the drawing room, to snuggle down into warmth, and to lie beside him—she caught her breath. She remembered the time in the hall when he had put his arms around her, simply to comfort her, no more, but her body had responded in a treacherous way. She had felt warm, and protected—and more, but difficult to define now. She only knew she had enjoyed that brief hug more than she should have. Far more. . . .

Back to the drawing room clutching the hot water bottle, back to see him already lying down, eyes closed, one lamp beside him on the floor, fire burning brightly, welcoming her back. She kicked off her slippers, took a deep breath and eased herself in. Her heart thudded so loudly she wondered if he heard it. But oh, it was warm! It was so warm——

'Why do you carry a sleeping bag with you?' she asked, because that was a normal question, and she needed to hang on to normality in this bizarre situation.

'It was in the boot of my car. It is always there, you understand. But when the snow began, and I went to cover the car with papers, I brought it in.' Both lay on their backs, side by side, not looking, not turning towards each other to speak.

'Because——' she had to clear her throat, 'because you thought we might need it?'

'Yes.'

She could not relax. This had been a mistake, she knew that now. He was too near, their bodies touched. A line of fire down her left side, a sharp bodily awareness. But warmth. Too much warmth. She wasn't tired now, she was vividly, blindingly aware of his total nearness. She could not close her eyes. He had extinguished the lamp, and the firelight danced on a darkened ceiling, bright images that dissolved and changed with each slow measured second that passed. 'You are tense,' he said. 'Relax. I have told you——'

'I know. You'll have to give me time. I've never done this before!' A feeble attempt at a joke.

'You have never slept with a man?' his voice seemed gently curious, no more, but she didn't want this subject, even though she had said those words.

Her voice was sharp, dismissive. 'I did not mean *that*——'

He turned his head then. 'I am sorry, I should not have asked——'

'No, you shouldn't.' She turned away from him, to lie on her side, and if he touched her, she was going to get out of that sleeping bag. She would not be able to bear it if he touched her——

Then she felt him moving, twisting round in the close confines of the large zipped-up bag, and she stiffened, back rigid, eyes wide. Please don't let him touch me— 'That is better. More comfortable. Sleep, Victoria. You are safe with me.' No hand came out, no arm came round her. His body curved to her back, but he kept his arms to himself, and she could feel his breath on her neck and she could see him as she had seen him on television that one unforgettable time, the magnificent figure leaping into space, soaring like a bird before plummeting down, down, the snow-covered mountain side. He lay behind her, not moving, as aware as she was of the difficulties of their situation, that incredible body, still now, not active, relaxed, ready to sleep. Or was he? Surely he was not blind?

And then—oh, surely she was imagining it? She heard his breathing change, deeper, go steady, and waited, waited, knew that it was not her imagination. He was asleep. Her own body began to relax, the warmth was too irresistible, gradually she found, despite her tensions, that sleep was taking over, her eyes were heavy, she could not think straight, images blurred. Then one picture came into her mind, just before she fell asleep. A picture of the attics at Drummell House, attics crammed with relics of the past, letters and books and photographs. They must look there tomorrow, tomorrow. . . .

When she awoke it was morning. Daylight peeped into the room through a chink in the curtains, a narrow shaft of sunlight in which motes of dust danced and sparkled. The room was icy chill, fire dead, but they were warm. And Gregor's arm lay across her body, caught in sleep, heavy and relaxed and unaware. She had actually slept!

Cautiously, Victoria felt in front of her for the zipper catch, and eased it down very slowly, and slid out of the bag. He didn't stir. His breathing didn't change, nor did he open his eyes. She crept out of the room and caught her breath as the chill air struck. How stupid she had been. She pulled a face at the memory of her own prudish behaviour, and determined to make amends, went into the kitchen and lit the gas. She would make tea and toast and take it into him in an unspoken apology. She lit a second ring, sliced his home-made bread and began toasting it. The smell was almost unbearably delicious and her stomach rumbled its protest, and the kettle began to boil, and her heart was lighter. A watery sun shone in through the window. It was another day, one more day beginning and soon there would be a thaw and the world would get back to normal.

She wanted a wash. She really wanted a bath, but that was impossible. The comforts of civilisation were never fully appreciated until they were gone, she thought. A bath had never been considered a luxury, but she yearned to sink into a warm tub, in a cosy bathroom—'Stop!' she said out loud. She would not think of baths any more. Rather of reality. And had the Victoria Mitchell of nearly two hundred years ago stood thus in this kitchen? Had the Gregor Shenkov of that time been also to Drummell House as this Gregor had done? She shivered in the cold of the room as though ghostly echoes of the past returned. As if she could reach out and touch. It had been weird and strange, that sensation she had experienced when Gregor had said the name of his own ancestor, his namesake. Gregor Shenkov and

Victoria Mitchell. Victoria Shenkov as she would have become, perhaps in the ancient church between Drummell House and the village. Of course! She must ask him where they had married. The church was over two hundred years old, there might be records. . . .

She snatched the toast away from the flame just in time and waved it to cool it before putting it on the plate. Victoria Shenkov. No—Shenkova—a final 'a' added in Russian surnames, that much she knew, for women.

She put margarine on the toast, and then marmalade, both of which were running short. No matter, there was jam, and cheese, until the shops could be reached. Her mind switched from dreaming to practicalities, from the distant past to the realities of their present situation, and there seemed no strangeness in that. She put tea and toast on a tray and carried it along towards the hall and she seemed to hear the rustle of silken gowns, the echo of distant laughter, and she smiled to herself. I should be a writer, with my imagination, she thought, and her steps faltered so that the crockery on the tray rattled. A writer—to write *that*, the history of her family, what a pleasure that would be!

How Uncle Craig would love it. She was already intrigued by all they had discovered in the past day or so. To clothe the facts in vivid colour would be something else. She had always loved Drummell House. It would be a fitting tribute to it, to write of the lives and loves of those who had lived in it for so many generations.

Nearly at the drawing room now. She balanced the tray while she opened the door, and as she did so, Gregor awoke, and looked up at her. 'Good morning,' he said.

'Good morning. No need to ask if you slept well.'

'No. And you?'

'Yes. I've made breakfast. It's in—apology——' she hesitated slightly over the word.

'There is no need. But thank you.' He sat up and rubbed his face. 'You must excuse me first.' He lifted back the covers and vanished out of the room. It was cold, so cold. Victoria raked the ashes out, put the rolled-up paper spills that she had made the previous day on to the remaining charred pieces of logs, carefully placed a few small twigs on top and lit them. Flames flickered and danced, and she put on two thin logs, and drew the fire with the large metal cover used for that purpose. As he returned, he was greeted by a fire, admittedly small, not yet hot, but cheerful. Both sat on the stools as close as possible and began to eat.

'There are many jobs to do,' he said, looking at the high pile of ashes waiting to be cleared. 'When we have eaten I will light the other fires——'

'And then we must go to the attics. I remembered last night, there are lots of old books and papers there.'

'Attics?' he frowned.

She searched for the word in French. *'Les greniers.'*

'Ah, oui, mais c'est bien possible——' He had replied instinctively in French, and she laughed, as did he after a moment. 'You speak French, Victoria?'

'A little, enough to get by when I'm there. The French appreciate it more, I find.'

'That is true. It is my home of course, but sometimes——' he looked towards the window, 'sometimes,' he went on, voice softer, 'I know that my heart is not there. When I am in the mountains, in the snow—there I feel an affinity.'

'Then—here——' She followed the direction of his glance at the snow outside. 'Do you also feel it here?'

He turned his head and looked at her. 'I felt it when I came here, and for me it was the first time in my life. I felt as if I was coming home.'

At his words, Victoria went still. That too was how she felt, and always had, always would. And something of the magic of the place had touched him, a stranger, an alien from somewhere so different. His face had gone very serious, almost sad. The urge to touch him almost overwhelmed, and tears sprang to her eyes. She supposed that in many ways, the harsh north of Scotland could remind him of his original home in Russia. For several moments neither spoke. They sat closely, and there was a stillness in the air, a waiting, almost as if they actually touched; a deep, wordless communication that went beyond anything she had ever known. It was most strange, this feeling she had, and she closed her eyes. She felt as if she knew all about him, as if in one moment, something had happened to let her see.

'Victoria?' His hand touched hers. A tingle as though at an electric shock ran up her arm, and she turned.

'Yes?' He took his hand away. Perhaps he too was aware of it. Nothing like this had ever happened to her before. It was as if they were surrounded by golden light, held in a misty gold that was as fragile as spun glass, as brittle . . . she had to move—she had to—she could not bear it a second longer. . . . Her heart thudded so loudly that she shook with the force of it. 'Yes?' she said again, voice a whisper, a thread of sound.

'That is how I felt,' he said, 'and I did not know why. And that was why it was a shock to me when I saw you.'

That didn't make sense. What did he mean? 'I don't—don't——'

'You said to me that it was as if I didn't want you here——'

She remembered, said in haste, forgotten, but remembered by him. 'Did I?' She was breathless.

'It was because—I had seen a picture of my ancestress, Victoria, once, long ago. A faded miniature, too fragile to bring with me—she looked exactly like you. It could have *been* you, Victoria, do you not see?'

It explained so much. And in a way, it was as if he was telling her something she already knew, had known from the first minute they met. A deep awareness, one that had so disturbed her, a fragile reaching out from the past—'I see,' she answered, voice so quiet that he had to lean over to hear her. She clasped her hands together to stop them from trembling. 'It looks,' she continued, in a voice that was far from steady, 'as though you and I might be related, doesn't it?'

'Yes.'

'Then—why don't we go and search the attics, and look for proof!'

'We will do so.'

'I had—when I was returning from the kitchen with our breakfast, I had a thought. It would be something rather wonderful, I decided, if I wrote a history of my family. Not for publication, you understand, but simply for my uncle, my parents and brother and sister to have.'

'And for yourself. You love it more than anyone else I think.'

'Yes, I do.' She could not sit still any longer, but went to the window to look out. And from behind her his voice came:

'You do not surprise me, saying that. For why do you think I came here?'

The trees outside, black outlines against white, had been there for over two hundred years. And now she knew that the other Victoria had stood at this same window. It was not supposition now, but knowledge. She had stood thus, looking out at smaller, thinner trees, but the *same ones*. And she felt Gregor moving behind her, and knew what would happen next. She was being held against him, was being enclosed tightly in a pair of strong arms, and she did not need to move away, she did not want to. She made a small wordless murmur of sound deep in her throat and felt his arms tighten. 'I came here,' he whispered in her ear, 'because I am writing the history of my family, for my father. That is what all the papers were that you saw. And now, do you realise, our stories will unite at one point—it will become one story.'

'And we are cousins,' she answered. 'Long ago, and far away, we have shared grandparents.'

'Yes.' And she turned, slowly because of the restraint of his arms. Turned so that she faced him, and was still held closely by him, and lifted her face to see his, and knew what he would do next, as if she had always known that too. And he kissed her. A long, lingering gentle kiss, sweet and soft, a kiss for cousins—or maybe for lovers. And then it was over and he moved, and she felt the rough bristles on her cheeks and made a low murmur of laughing protest, and put her hand up. 'You need a shave,' she whispered.

'So I do.' But he did not release her. His fingers on her back moved slowly, sensuously. She was caught in a blur of mindless awareness, physical sensation that floated her away. Eyes closed, she clung to him, feeling the hard muscles of his back beneath her hands, revelling in his strength, wanting desperately for him to kiss her again. But he did not. Instead he released her, held her away from him, eyes darkened, strangely shadowed, mouth serious. 'It is better not,' he said.

Her breathing was rapid. Eyes met, in them the unspoken message, old as time. She knew, they both knew. It was not only a kiss; it had been far more than that. 'Yes,' she answered. 'I know.' And he turned away, walked back to the fire, bent and placed more logs on the rapidly growing flames. She watched him, watched every move, remained by the window, although it was cold.

'I should not have kissed you,' he said. 'I did not intend that to happen.'

'Do you wish you hadn't?'

'No.' He straightened up slowly, dusting his hands from the wood. 'But we are alone here, Victoria, and will be for some days more, I think.' The bright sharp edge of awareness touched them both. She felt as though she had melted inside, she felt—strange; something rich and wonderful happening to her—and she understood it only too well. She knew that she wanted Gregor to make

love to her. In her heart she knew already how it
would be, and in her mind. The desire for him
throbbed like a pain—and she watched him, and
said nothing because she could not speak. She had
wanted only one man before—Peter. Had wanted
him so much that they had planned a weekend
together in the cottage of an old friend of Victoria's.
The plans had been made, she had bought herself a
beautiful négligé and nightdress in readiness—she
was packing it when the phone call that had
shattered her love for him into a thousand pieces had
come. That one fateful call, from a cousin, to say
that Peter was married. She had given the nightdress
and négligé away, unable to look at them again. Oh
yes, she thought, watching him as he began to move
the books—I know what longing is, I know what it is
to want somebody—and he turned as if her thoughts
had reached him, and came over to her, to stand
before her, this time hands at sides.

'What are you thinking?' he asked.

'Don't you know? I thought you could read my
mind?'

He smiled slightly. 'I sense you are troubled. I
do not read your thoughts.'

'The man you reminded me of—I was thinking
of him.'

'Because we kissed? Is that why?'

'Partly.' She could never tell him.

'I did not do it to remind you——'

'I know that,' she cut him off. 'It doesn't matter.
He's not important any more.'

'But he was.'

'Once. Yes, he was.' She didn't want to talk any
more. Her mouth had gone dry. 'It's—over——'
She made a dismissive gesture with her hand.

'Did you love him very much?'

'I don't want to *talk* about him!' She gasped, then, without thinking: 'Haven't you ever loved a woman very much?'

There was a stillness. A waiting pause. 'I have made love to several—I have never loved any.' It was a brutally honest answer and she felt herself stiffen in shock. If he had intended to shock her, he could have done no better.

'Thank you for your frankness,' she said. 'I'm not like *you* then.'

'Ask me *why*?' he said, and took her arm.

'Why? What? Why you've made love to so many women—or why you've never loved any?' she whispered. His grip was hard. She could not move away.

'Why I have never loved any,' he said.

'Why then?' But she didn't want to know, not really—or did she? She wasn't sure any more.

'Because I have been searching for one special woman, all my life.'

'You may never find her. You may waste your life searching.'

'Is that what you think?'

'It's what I'm sure of. I thought that with him— with Peter. He was everything I'd always wanted, and more.' She tried to move away. 'Please let me go.'

He released her on the instant, but she didn't move. The atmosphere was strange, heady, almost as though she had been drinking. She felt light headed, most odd. 'I suppose you met many women in your travels.' She was hungry for knowledge, now, as if she needed to know all she could about this, her—cousin. That was stranger still. In a way they shared the same blood. Well-mingled with others, over the years, but at one time, far, far back, there had been the blood link. 'I suppose they wanted to be seen with a star like you.'

'I hope they wanted me for myself.' There was a glint in his eyes, hard to decide of what, almost as if of mockery. A glint of mockery, and a slight curve to his mouth. 'But yes—I have known many.'

The mockery stung her. 'Well, good for *you*. I'll bet they just *fling* yourselves in your arms!'

'Some of them—yes.'

'Well *I* won't, never fear!' Thank God, *that* had brought her back to earth with a bump. Any slight traces of dizzy longing had vanished like mist. She felt angry with him more than anything else.

'I know that, Victoria.' He stroked her cheek, the mockery had gone. 'But nothing that is worth having is ever easy. I am sure you know that.'

Oh yes, she knew what he meant. Was that why Peter had been so absolutely shattered when she had told him she knew the truth? Because he had been trying to persuade her into bed with him for seven months, and had all but succeeded? She knocked Gregor's hand away. She had been mistaken. They *were* alike. She shivered. She had had a lucky escape from Peter. She had nearly made a fool of herself—if only in the secret recesses of her mind—with Gregor. Never again. He would regret it if he kissed her, or attempted to, again. She took a deep breath.

'We have work to do,' she said crisply. 'Suppose we light the fires first and then get our coats on?'

'Coats?' he repeated, puzzled.

'For the attics,' she said. 'You know—*les greniers*. It will be very cold up there.' She even managed a little smile. Not as mocking as his, but slightly superior nevertheless. He nodded.

'Of course. I will do the fires. You may care to move *our bed* away from here while I do so.' Had she imagined the faintest emphasis on the words 'our bed'? She decided to ignore it anyway.

'Fine,' she agreed. 'Just fine.' But as he left the room she stared after him. He was a deeply complex creature. He puzzled her. He also intrigued her far more than she was prepared to admit even to herself. He was, without any doubt, a strangely fascinating man.

CHAPTER SEVEN

THEY spent all of the morning in the attics. No wonder Uncle Craig never comes up here, she thought, as she surveyed the results of their combined efforts just before lunchtime. It would take weeks to properly assess the contents of those four huge rooms let alone go through everything. They had made a good start, had chosen the first, largest attic to be the repository of everything that could prove valuable for their purpose. Already the effort showed. Several cartons of books were stacked neatly along one wall, a suitcase full of old photographs had been rooted out by Gregor and put alongside the books.

But there was so much more to search through. The dust of years lay over everything. Trunks of faded clothes, an old rocking horse that Victoria remembered with affection, pictures, some framed, some not, chairs awaiting repair—chests of drawers crammed with the debris of more than two hundred years—all there, waiting for someone as mad enough as her to come along and disturb it. She wiped a grimy hand across her forehead and sneezed as dust tickled her nostrils. 'Oh. That's it for now. I'm hungry.'

'Then we will carry these down—make room for whatever else we find later,' said Gregor, surveying their booty with satisfaction.

'Fine.' She wasn't going to argue. Things would be kept on this impersonal level and all would be well. *It had* to be. The sleeping arrangements would be the same tonight as the previous one. . . .

He handed her a smaller box of dusty volumes and then picked up two boxes, one on top of the other. 'I will return for the rest while you prepare our meal,' he told her. Victoria went ahead without replying, walking carefully down the steeper attic stairs. Those rooms could tell some tales. They had once been occupied by servants, long ago. And ghostly yarns would have been spun by the light of flickering candles, she could almost see it. She smiled to herself at her fancies. Nearly there now. She was no longer cold. The exertion had warmed them both, and certainly given her an appetite.

They left the cartons in the drawing room which was, she thought, in some slight dismay, coming to resemble a camp sight, with mattress and sleeping bag, and now these. And Uncle Craig wouldn't give a damn, would probably join in whole-heartedly. She had to smile at that too.

Lunch, the last four eggs made into a large omelette with *fines herbes*, and bread, and coffee, was satisfying, and as she cleared away the plates, she said: 'Ready when you are.'

'I have been thinking,' he said. 'We have neither of us washed properly since yesterday——'

'Well, it's a bit difficult, isn't it?' she said dryly.

'We could do it out here, this evening.' A pause. 'Separately, of course.' Ironically that last.

'Have a *bath*?'

'No. But heat up sufficient water to have an — ' he shrugged, 'an adequate substitute.'

It was not only a good idea, she wondered why she hadn't thought of it herself. 'Yes,' she agreed.

'You're right. The kitchen will be warm if we keep the stove on—it's a brilliant idea, Gregor.'

He nodded. 'Yes. I know,' and she glanced at him. She would make sure the door was secured before she had hers. They had gone across to fetch more logs before going up to the attics, and outside the air froze the breath, hurt the skin. There was no sign of a thaw. And if the water froze in the pipes, as was eminently possible, then even that simple form of ablution would be difficult.

She was glad in a way that Uncle Craig was in hospital. Although fit, he was no longer a young man, and if he had been on his own, he would have had difficulty managing. 'There must be something we can do,' she said, more to herself, in thought, and Gregor, about to leave the room, paused.

'About what?' he asked.

'I was thinking – Uncle Craig could easily have been here on his own in weather like this. I'm glad he's not. It's not easy for us, and we're a lot younger - —'

'I too have considered that. The central heating for a start is not adequate for a house this size. He should get it renewed, should also have an alternative form of lighting for when the electricity is cut off——'

'It's easier said than done,' she remarked.

'Nothing is impossible,' he said softly. 'The windows are not double glazed. That is necessary too I think——'

'He's getting old, Gregor, he's happy as he is. I just worry about times like this.' She was stung by the assurance in his tone, which was stupid of her, she knew, for he was being helpful. He just didn't realise——

'As I would if I were you.' He paused. 'It would be better if he did not live alone.'

'He has a housekeeper who comes in every day from the village——'

'No. I mean someone to live here, with him. Have *you* ever thought of it?'

'Me?' she gasped. How very odd it was that he should say that. How very strange indeed. It had been a recurring dream for years with Victoria that one day she would live at Drummell, a certain inner conviction, repeated in so many dreams— but why had he said it? Why? 'What made you say that?' Her heart skipped a beat. He said he could not read her mind, but he had the disconcerting habit of echoing her secret thoughts.

He shrugged. 'I see you here,' he answered simply, and the words seemed to resound strangely in her ears. I see you here, I *see* you *here*——

'Because I *am* here,' she said, more to blot out the echo than anything.

'Yes. Now. Of course. But——' he paused and looked at her, those green eyes startling in their inner vision, brilliant eyes looking out from a shrewd and brilliant mind.

'But?' she queried, soft lest it disturb his train of thought.

'But that was not what I meant. I can see you here with a family—a husband—and children.' He looked round the kitchen, his eyes distant, as if he did not really see the room, only something beyond, and she felt a frisson run up her spine. What did *he* see, this man? Ghosts of the future while she saw only those of the past? He grew more disturbing by the minute, and to break the unbearable tension that had grown so suddenly, she laughed.

'Do you read fortunes as well?'

He turned his eyes steadily back to her. They saw too much, those eyes. The briefest flicker of a smile touched his mouth. 'I can tell you are amused, Victoria. Perhaps you are right. It is just that you belong here. And I think you know it as well.' And he turned and went out. For an exit line it could not be beaten. She did belong here. She had always known it.

She followed him very slowly, more shaken than she would admit, up to the attic, walking softly, hearing him moving boxes, whistling an old pop tune, and went in to see him on his haunches lifting out yet more books, this time from a battered trunk. He looked up. Dirt was smudged down one cheek and this, together with his darkly unshaven jaws and cheeks, lent him a piratical appearance. He only needs an eye patch, she thought, and he'd look terrifying. The wash, this evening, would not be before time, and she sighed at the thought, and he, misunderstanding the sigh, said: 'You wish to leave these today?'

She went and crouched beside him. 'I wasn't sighing about the work. I was sighing in longing for a good wash.'

'Ah. I see.' He grinned, and there was something almost boyish about him just for a moment. She could see for an instant why so many women would find him attractive. She wished she didn't.

'What have you here?' she asked hastily, and her hand brushed his as she delved into the trunk and she jerked it away. 'Oh! There's nothing much here—I think this was a job lot my uncle bought at a house sale——'

'Job lot? What is that?'

'Er—a trunkful of books—this—that he would buy cheaply, without seeing.'

'I understand—I think. Okay. We close this.' He did so, snapping the lid down briskly, and stood up. Victoria followed suit.

'Look, I'll go and look through that chest over there. Can you see if there's anything in that cupboard?'

'Yes, of course.' And so, for the next hour or so, they worked separately, he bringing her an occasional interesting looking book over, either to be dismissed by Victoria, or added to the pile in the first attic. Eventually he said, 'See—the light is fading. I think, Victoria, we must leave this for today, and return in the morning.'

'There's so much——' she gestured round her.

'Yes. Come, let us go.'

'You're right.' It was suddenly dusk, all shadows, and she moved away quickly from him, not wanting to be too near, and caught her foot on a concealed toy and stumbled. He held her arm.

'Be careful, Victoria.'

'Yes. I must——' He released her arm, and it tingled. She wanted to escape, and she had had that feeling before but never so strongly.

'I will go first down the stairs.' In case I fall, you mean, she thought, but she did not say it. She followed him down and both went into the kitchen, which was comparatively warm. The kettle was put on, tea pot warmed ready for a hot drink. He began to wipe round the sink. 'You shall wash first,' he told her. 'Then I will—and then we will eat. I will prepare a thick meat broth and we shall eat it with *croutons*, and that will be warming for us.' Even as he spoke he was leaving the room to go to the freezer, which, Victoria reckoned, being in the laundry room by the back door to the stable yard, was as effective switched off as on in this weather.

There was a clothes horse in the pantry. She took that out and at his questioning gaze as he returned, explained: 'We can leave this near the hall fire—I'm going to wash some—er—smalls.'

He seemed about to ask what she meant by 'smalls', then smiled. 'A good idea,' was his only comment. She carried it through, placed it near but not near enough to fall on the hall fire and went upstairs for clean clothes. Returning, she took off her coat, and left that on a chair in the hall. She had deliberately put out of her mind his remarks of before, but now, as she stood in the hall looking out towards his car, they returned to her. 'You belong here.' She repeated his words softly to herself. Her career meant a great deal to her—but Drummell, and all that it stood for, meant far more. The germ of an idea had taken root, and like everything that was a basic truth, refused to go away. She supposed subconsciously that it had been one of her reasons for inviting Peter to stay with her there—only she hadn't known then that he had a wife tucked away in Lincolnshire. She had hoped he would love it as much as she—only he hadn't. He hadn't made it obvious, he was too clever for that. He had marvelled at the beauty of the house, had walked round the gardens on a summer evening with her and kissed her, and told her that he loved her very much. But he couldn't wait to fly back to London when the Monday came. She wondered now, with the benefit of hindsight, whether Uncle Craig had actually *liked* him at all. He welcomed all her friends with equal enthusiasm—but Victoria had been faintly uneasy all the while the visit lasted, and now could see what she hadn't before seen. She took a deep breath. She had made an absolute fool of herself over Peter. She would not do so again in a hurry.

But still, if she was going to write a history of Drummell and its occupants, would here not be the perfect place to do so? She was less than three hours away from London by plane. . . . Thoughts formed, took shape, became more solid, and a small sense of excitement grew within her. There would be continuation—and Uncle Craig would be happy—and that was as important as anything else. He was so near, yet so far. She wanted, above all, to discuss the idea with him. She rubbed her arms, lost in reverie and turned at the sound of Gregor's voice.

'Victoria? Ah—you are here. There is water ready.'

'Oh. Sorry. I was miles away. Thank you.' She picked up towel and clothes and followed him back into the kitchen. The sink was full of hot steaming water, the kettle bubbled on the stove, and a covered pan simmered. Gregor had remained by the door, hand on handle.

'Call me when you have finished. After I have washed and shaved, we will have our evening meal.'

'Yes.' She waited until he was well gone, pushed a stool under the door handle and began to strip off. She did not consider for one moment that he would return before she called, but it made her feel more secure. The hot water was bliss, even though it wasn't a bath and as she flannelled herself vigorously she considered calor gas heaters for the bathrooms in cold such as this. Portable, independent of mains gas or electricity—a distinct possibility and one she felt sure Uncle Craig would never have even thought about. There was so much that could be done, given time. It was part of her heritage, this wonderful old house, in her blood. . . .

Skin tingling, she dressed in clean underwear, clean pullover, same jeans, and refilled both sink and kettle ready for Gregor. Then she went to the door and opened it. He came out of the drawing room when she called, carrying a towel-wrapped bundle. She had draped newly washed bra, pants and socks over the clothes horse, and they steamed gently in the heat from the fire. She added the towel as an afterthought and went into the drawing room to wait. Irresistible images came to mind and refused to go away. Images of Gregor standing stripped in the kitchen by the sink, dripping on to the newspaper-covered floor, scrubbing himself, perhaps whistling, or singing as he shaved; he would look magnificent, she knew. He would have a hard muscular body, long legs— she took a deep breath. And that's enough, she thought. That is *quite* enough. Thoughts like that—she took another deep breath. Had he thought of *her* thus? Had his imagination roved?

She knelt by the fire and combed her silky long hair, eyes half closed, dreaming, drifting, thoughts warm. And so might she sit thus in a few months, or years—she could grow old here, she knew. She could spend her life here. She recalled Gregor's words with soft surprise—I can see you here with a family—a husband—and children. And so can I, she thought. One day, one day. She would not marry a man who did not love Drummell as much as she did. It was a house meant for children to live in, to slide squealing down the banisters she herself had slid down as a child, to explore the attics and cellars and play hide and seek, as she and her brother and sister and friends had in those days long ago. To run about in the gardens, see the rabbits and watch the birds through binoculars. Sometimes an eagle soared overhead, and deer wandered down from the mountains. . . . There would be food dropped from helicopters for them, and if we cut a large S.O.S. in the snow, a helicopter would land here—she sat on her heels and thought about that, and then closed her eyes. No. Not yet. When the snow went, it would be different. But—until then, in spite of the inconveniences, she could not, would not, leave. The house could not be abandoned like that. She shivered at the thought, and in the deepest recesses of her mind, perhaps another reason lurked, but one not even to be thought about. There was some magic afoot of which she was not consciously aware, and that magic had to do with Gregor's presence. For she sensed that he, too, belonged here, in some strange way.

She heard his voice calling her and scrambled to her feet, pushing the comb in her bag and flinging it on the chair. She was not aware of the bag falling to the carpet, for it made no sound. It fell—and opened, the contents spilling out. And there it remained until they returned after their meal. It was Gregor who saw it first. Victoria was deciding that the low table might be a better place for the lamp, and was trying it there when he spoke.

'Your handbag has fallen, Victoria.' She was getting used to hearing her name spoken by him now, and turned to see him pointing.

'Oh. Thank you.' She knelt, as he did, and began to retrieve the scattered contents, blushing at the mess—lipstick, comb, paper handkerchiefs—two pens—diary—purse—coins scattered as well. She had meant to clean it out before she came, had been meaning to for months. Oh shame, oh embarrassment!

'And this, I think also.' And her heart stopped for a second. He was holding a photograph, was standing up, moving nearer to the lamp.

'Please——' she held out her hand. She had *forgotten* that. The one photograph of Peter, tucked away—totally forgotten. She stood up, went over. 'Please, Gregor,' she said. He looked up from it, face hard and serious.

'This is Peter,' he said, and he wasn't asking—he was telling her.

'Yes. Please give it to me.'

'You kept it?' His voice was deeper, strange that, the accent stronger as well, harsher.

'I *forgot* it.'

'He does not look very much like me——'

'It's a bad photo. I—I don't know why it's still there, will you please give it back to me? I want to throw it away——' she was babbling, angry and upset and dismayed, all in one awful mixture and she tried to take it from him but he held his hand away, turned his back to her and looked closely at it again. Then, turning, he gave it to her. She didn't even look at it, just tore it in two and flung it into the flames to see it swallowed instantly.

'And he was your lover?'

'That's none of your business!' she snapped.

'True.' He shrugged, but his eyes were curiously intent. They saw everything, missed nothing. 'But I have told you——'

'You've told me *nothing*!' she said shortly.

'Then which do you want to hear about? The French actress? Or the American heiress—or——' He got no further. Angry beyond all sense or understanding, Victoria silenced him by slapping him hard. Aghast at what she had done—not even sure why, she stood there wide eyed, trembling, her face ashen.

And he began to *laugh*. He threw back his head and laughed, then, so suddenly that it took her completely by surprise, he caught her and held her, looked down at her, eyes glinting devilishly, and said:

'Never do that to me again.'

'Let me *go*!' she shouted, and stamped on his foot. She had been about to apologise. His action had cancelled that. She struggled to be free, and he released her.

'Little wildcat,' he taunted. 'What a *temper* you have!'

She was still trembling with spent rage. And shocked at the force of her own reaction. She did not understand it. Without another word, because she could not bear to be in the same room with him any longer, she whirled round and ran out. She went into the kitchen and slammed the door behind her, sat down at the table and began to take deep breaths, brushing her hair back from her face. What on earth had happened? She put her hand to her mouth.

The kitchen was in darkness, and growing cooler. She looked towards the window and out, seeking an answer but there was none. She had behaved in a stupid and childish way because he had found a photograph, and then asked her—she took a deep breath. No, that wasn't why she had struck him. She had hit him in hard deep anger because he had spoken of *his* lovers—and she had not been able to bear it for a moment longer. It was cold, she was cold. She lit the gas under the kettle and waited for it to boil, shivering in the darkness. How could she face him again?

She filled a beaker with boiling water and spooned in coffee powder. His voice came quietly from behind her and she whirled round, startled.

'Is there a drink for me?' She saw only the black outline of him. The air was grey, everything grainy, as in an old photograph. She could not see his expression. She did not know if he was angry, or mocking, or upset, for his voice gave nothing away. And perhaps now was the time to apologise, now, when neither could see, or be seen.

'Yes. I'll make you one. I'm sorry, Gregor. I don't know why I hit you.' There, she'd said it, and felt slightly better.

'Do you not?' he said, a curious answer. 'I have forgotten it. Come, let us return to where it is warm.' No, he wasn't angry, if he ever had been. He took the beaker from her, hands warm, touching hers lightly, and she filled a second one, and her thoughts were confused. She wanted—no, she didn't know what she wanted. She felt unhappy, and she wanted to cry, and she wasn't going to do that, not now, not here.

He opened the door for her and led her through, one arm across her shoulders as though he guided a child. And he spoke softly. 'It is difficult for two strangers to be alone under these conditions, I understand that.'

Strangers? Yes, they were, of course they were. But she didn't need sympathy from him. 'It would be difficult even if we were old friends,' she answered.

'That is true as well.' He opened the drawing-room door and here it was warm, and with light. Here he could see her face, and maybe he would know what troubled her. Everything was ready. After she had gone he must have unpacked the books and set them out. The case of photographs was on the chair by her handbag. If she hadn't combed her hair, none of this would have happened.

They sat on the footstools and he began leafing through the top book, and Victoria watched him, his head bent, intent on his search, and she sipped her hot black coffee, and she could not take her eyes from him. And she began to understand, at last, why she had hit him. She had never been jealous of anyone before, had never suffered those agonising pangs, and the emotion was an unfamiliar one, and it hurt. A French actress, an American heiress—how many more would she have heard if she had not stopped him? A dozen? More? She shuddered—and he looked up at her.

'Are you still cold?' he asked.

'No.' I wasn't shivering with cold, she thought, I had discovered something about myself, and it hurts. And in a few hours I'm going to sleep with you in the close, warm, confines of a large sleeping bag, and I don't know how I'll be able to bear that either, and her body ached to hold him, to be held by him, and she looked away from him and into the dancing flames. Oh dear lord, she thought, how can I love him? I don't know him. I wish I had never come—and even as that wish came, she knew it was not true. What she was experiencing now was richer by far than anything else that had ever happened to her in her life. It was time for work, not thought. She picked up a second book and began to riffle through the pages. It was a history of Scotland. In the index at the back, the name Mitchell—but no one known to her, not even remotely connected. If only she could remember where she had seen that walnut box. She put the book down to one side ready to be taken up again, and reached for the photographs. What she hoped to find there she was not sure, for there would be no photo before about 1850, if any then. But, she supposed, she was seeking a family resemblance, something to show Gregor—and she found it.

It was buried deep at the bottom of the box, below the newer snaps taken over the years—she and her parents, brother and sister taken on an early holiday. Her image looked out at her, and she smiled. She had long plaits then, and a gap in her teeth, white socks and flowered dress, grinning out at the camera. She laughed and Gregor took the snap from her, and asked: 'This is you?' pointing at her.

'Yes, with my parents, sister Anne and brother Michael. It was taken outside this window by my uncle.' There were more, they both looked, she smiling, explaining, remembering happy times. Then there were her grandparents, other snaps getting less informal all the time. It was as if the years lay in layers in the box, lifting and looking, going deeper and further back into the past. And always in the background, some aspect of Drummell House, until—there in a large envelope were others, faded, stiffly formal pictures posed in front of an artificial background that owed nothing to real life. An improbable garden, and painted trees, and the photographer's name engraved in one corner.

She read out loud as she passed them to him from the names on the back. 'My great-grandparents—his name was John, hers Anne— taken about 1890——' she looked at the back of the next one, and began to read. 'Andrew and Charlotte Mitchell with daughter Charlotte Victoria 1855——' and turned the photo over. She caught her breath. Looking out at the faded sepia coloured picture was a bearded man, strikingly handsome—just like her father; a pretty woman with a sweet smile, and a girl. The girl might have been Victoria herself, when younger. She felt rather than saw Gregor move, and he said:

'May I see?' And he was beside her.

'Yes. Those are my great-great grandparents— with their daughter, Charlotte Victoria, who would be my great-great aunt.' And she waited, and knew that the resemblance had struck him as forcibly, if not more so, as her. She heard his sharp intake of breath. In a not very steady voice, she went on: 'She would be the other Victoria's great niece.'

'She is——' he paused. 'She could be the woman in my picture—she could also be you when you were younger.'

'Yes. I know,' she said quietly. 'It remains only to go through the church records when the snow is gone and I think we will find the final proof we need.'

'If only I could tell my father now,' he said quietly.

'You will be able to, when the phones are working again. Uncle Craig will be surprised too.'

'They are such old friends. To know that they are also related——' Of course! She hadn't thought of that, simply of hers and Gregor's distant kinship. But Craig and Ivan were even closer. She marvelled at the quirk of fate—a mutual love of books—which had caused them to meet. The world was a strange place, and coincidences like this happened. Not, perhaps, too often, but just occasionally, and with the same stunning impact. She looked at him, crouched beside her, and a wonderful sense of well being filled her. He reached out, took her hand, and kissed it. 'Greetings, cousin,' he said, as he smiled.

CHAPTER EIGHT

EVERYTHING had changed, very subtly, a shifting of awareness, a fine drawn tension that filled everywhere, that made even normal conversation different. Because soon, they would go to bed. It was late, very late, the hours of the day stretched behind them, and before them lay the night. And now Victoria knew something that he did not—and she knew there was no way she could share a bed with him and sleep. Her skin tingled as though her nerve ends were afire. She was blindingly aware of his every move, every word. And he, too, was different. After that half-joking kiss on her hand, it was as if he too, had changed. There was something electric in the very air they breathed, yet on the surface, to an unobservant outsider perhaps nothing had altered. They had continued their search through books, Gregor had taken the box of snaps and looked at each one as if he found everything about Drummell of intense fascination, had asked her occasionally who this or that photo was of, had listened when she told him. Had carefully avoided touching her. The hour could not much longer be delayed. The distant chimes of the grandfather clock sounded midnight, and Victoria was desperately tired—yet equally desperately wide awake.

Then he spoke, shattering a silence that had gone on for too long. 'I think that tonight I will sleep on a settee,' he said.

She looked up from reading—but not really taking in—a history of old Aberdeen. Of course she knew why. She didn't have to ask. 'Sleep on the mattress,' she said. 'I can double the sleeping bag over. If you fetch a duvet down——'

'Yes. That will do.' Their eyes met. No words were needed. None said. He rose to his feet and went out silently, and Victoria began to move the chairs back to make more space. Had she then given herself away? No, she cried silently. She piled several logs on to the already blazing fire and stacked books and photographs on the table. Her limbs were heavy and it was difficult to move, and her mouth was dry. Had she only known him for four days? In another four, or five, he might be gone. He was going to Aviemore for some skiing, and then where, she wondered? Back to France? To send a Christmas card once a year—or a postcard from some exotic spot—there would be a woman waiting for him, some woman to whom he would tell his adventures in Scotland, and one day, because he felt at home here, he might bring one of them to see the house, and Victoria would be there, and would welcome him, and shake hands, and meet his mistress—or his wife—and would be the perfect hostess. She bit her lip. Then too, when—if—he returned, she might be married, with children, and he might remind her of his joking prophecy, and ask her if she remembered their days snowbound—and she would laugh and say, of course, how could she forget? And it would all be very civilised. . . .

'Shall we have a drink of hot chocolate?' His voice interrupted her thoughts.

'Yes. I'll make it.' He was carrying a duvet, an

extra pillow, and laid them down by the hearth to warm, and she watched him and said: 'Is there someone waiting for you in Paris?' and she hadn't intended to say it, and heard the words coming out, horrified, but it was too late.

He straightened up. 'Do you mean, is there a *woman* waiting for me?'

'I—don't know what made me say——' she began.

'But you did. Yes, there is. Why did you ask?'

'I don't know. I—thought she might be worried.' A feeble lie. It even sounded weak to her own ears.

'She will not be worried. She *knows* me.'

'So you're always off, travelling, are you?'

'I have been—yes.' He was watching her, not exactly smiling, but not making it any easier for her either, and she shrugged.

'And you, Victoria. Is there—*someone*—waiting for you, in London?'

'Oh yes! Heavens, yes!' That wasn't a lie. There was always someone, but never anyone important. There was Simon, and David—and Robert, good friends, no more than that.

'And is he worried?'

'I doubt it.' She even managed a laugh. '*He* knows *me*.'

'So, you are always off travelling too, are you?' A mockery of her own words, almost an exact copy, faintly but deliberately ironic.

'No. I work in the one place.' She turned and knelt to the sleeping bag—*her* sleeping bag now, and tucked the other half underneath to pad it. What was she like, this woman of his? Tall—petite—fair—dark? She wanted desperately to know, the desire gnawing at her heart in a raw pain. He didn't love her because he had said—but she might love him, might have her dreams. She might turn out to be the one for whom he searched, and if not her, then the next, or the next. . . . He could go on looking all his life. Look at me, she wanted to say. *Look at me*—but she didn't. She had to bite her tongue to stop herself from saying it, and concentrated on neatly folding the sleeping bag, corners just so——

'I remember, you told me. Do you enjoy your work?'

'Very much.' She could look up then, still kneeling, her hair loose about her face, the firelight and lamp soft upon her, unknowing of the picture she made at that moment and unaware of his reaction to it, because his eyes gave nothing away. His face was expressionless as he said:

'But you would leave it, and your family, to come up here?' The strange questions he asked, as if it mattered to him.

'Yes, I think I would. It wouldn't be "leaving" them. We are a very close famiy. They would be happy, knowing it is what I want. I have to thank you for that, Gregor.' Tears sparkled her eyes but she was unaware of them. He saw—but she only was aware of the tremor that touched his features for an instant, and it was almost of pain.

'You would have known, yourself, eventually. Perhaps I made you see sooner. That is all.'

'What is it?' she whispered, for he had closed his eyes, and stood there, and something about him distressed her in her new found, hopeless love.

'You have a home. Your roots are here. I can never return to my birthplace.' She rose slowly to her feet and walked across to him, her distress stronger than those other emotions conflicting inside her. Without thinking, only knowing that it was right, she put her arms around him as a mother might to a child.

'I am so sorry,' she whispered. 'I can't imagine how that must feel—but I am truly sorry.'

'Thank you.' He seemed to hesitate, then his arms went slowly around her, and for timeless moments they clung to one another. Her body filled with energy, as though she were the strong one. Idiotic really, he was so much bigger than her, so much more powerful but at that moment, all jealousy cast aside, she gave herself to him, and he responded. I love you, she thought, and I will miss you terribly when you go, even though I know this is impossible, we are worlds apart, and always will be, but here, now, we are together. And she moved slightly, easing herself free of his arms, and looked up at him and gave him her most gentle smile.

'Sit down, Gregor. I'll go and make that drink, and then, if you want to talk, we will. If you don't, we'll just have our chocolate and sit by the fire.' She squeezed his arms. 'Go on, sit down.'

'*Da, babushka,*' he said, and she half frowned, half laughed.

'Yes, little mother?' she queried, remembering something she had once read.

'Something like that. You speak my native tongue as well.' He had changed now, the dark momentary sadness gone, lightened with her words. She shook her head.

'No. But occasionally words stick. I won't be long,' and she went out. When she returned with two full beakers of lovely foaming hot chocolate— she had taken special care—he was sitting by the fire on a stool, looking into the flames. She knelt beside him and handed him a beaker. 'Would you like one of your cigars?' she asked him.

'The smell would linger.'

'It doesn't matter! Uncle Craig smokes them all the time. Where are they?'

'On the sideboard over there. I will——'

'Stay there.' She put her cup down and went to fetch one, handed it to him and found a half-burned twig which she thrust into the heart of the fire. Kneeling again beside him, she held it to the end of the cigar. She was vividly conscious of every movement made by both of them, brightly *aware* of everything as if every moment was to be savoured, was infinitely wonderful. There is only now, and here, for us. There is no one else, can not be for this day and whatever days that we have left, and this is a special time for me, and perhaps for him too, a brief interlude from the world he knows. And I will have this memory and others, for as long as I live, and somewhere, long ago, our namesakes shared time as well. And that added a fine piquancy to everything. He had bent his head, his hands touched hers holding the twig. It was like the circuit in an electric current being completed, a buzz so strong that it took her breath away, but not by a flicker did she move, until the cigar glowed red, and she flung the twig from her and picked up her drink.

'Do you want to talk?' she asked softly.

He shook his head. 'Not—now. One day, perhaps.'

But there wouldn't be a 'one day'. She took a deep breath. 'Of course. I understand. Tell me, shall we search for the walnut box tomorrow?'

'Yes. I am intrigued, Victoria.' His eyes caught and held hers, and he smiled. 'You must not be offended that I do not wish to talk of certain things. It is just that——' he hesitated. 'Some things go too deep to speak about.'

'Truly, I understand.' Eyes bright, she regarded him. 'It is late anyway. We're both tired.'

'Yes. That is true.' He looked at his beaker. 'I shall never again drink hot chocolate without thinking of Drummell House.'

'Oh! Not of me?' she said lightly.

'And of you—of course,' he added. 'But then, how could I think of one and not the other?'

'How indeed,' she agreed, and she didn't want to talk any more. She wished vainly that she had a sleeping pill. Or even knock out drops or a Mickey Finn, as in all the best detective films, she thought, wryly. *Anything* to help me sleep. She finished her drink. 'Well, that's me for bed.' She gave a realistic yawn. 'Gosh, I'm tired.'

'Yes. So am I.' He took the beakers and went out with them, and Victoria looked doubtfully at the sleeping bag, pulled a face, and slid slowly in and zipped herself up. As she was going to be awake for sometime, she decided, she might as well begin mentally writing her book. Where would she start? 'There have always been Mitchells at Drummell House. It was built in 1750 by Alexander Mitchell. . . .'

It would do. She heard him returning, closing the door, then the light went out, and she heard his movements, bright sparks flew up the chimney with the thud of logs going on the fire, the duvet being shaken, then: 'Goodnight, Victoria.'

'Goodnight, Gregor.' Back to work in her mind,

concentrate on that and nothing else. 'Alexander Mitchell who owned vast tracts of land in what is now the Grampian Region. . . .' But *why* had he suggested this? Did he feel as she did? Was he also afraid—that was ridiculous. A man who had had a French heiress and an American actress—no, hang on, that wasn't right, it was the other way round—*and* some unknown waiting for him. Waiting indeed, why hadn't she come with him? Uncle Craig would have welcomed them both—only then there would have been three people. Victoria pulled a face. It would not have been the same, most definitely not the same . . . goodnight, cousin, she thought. I'm writing my book you know, in my head because it's more fun than lying awake just thinking of you—dear God, I wish he was holding me now. Just holding me, nothing else, just holding me as I held him before. I want him, I want him so much, and he will never know, and in a way I wish he did, oh lord, how I wish he did.

She closed her eyes, and tears came, large silent tears that fell on her pillow, and she could taste them, salt, and she clenched her mouth to stifle any sobs, desperately afraid he would hear, which made it worse. . . .

'Victoria?' He was sitting up. She saw the blurred outline. She didn't answer because her voice would have betrayed her. And she saw him *move*, and froze.

He knelt beside her. 'Victoria—you are weeping.'

'No—I—I'm——' her voice was choked, muffled into the pillow. The next moment she was being lifted, being cradled in a pair of powerful, but oh, so gentle arms. And the tears came freely then, as if released from silence.

'Oh, my darling, do not cry,' he said. 'Do not cry——' He held her so closely, so warmly, he cradled her in his arms, and laid his cheek against hers, stroking her hair, rocking her gently against his chest. Then, he murmured: 'One moment,' and vanished to return with his duvet which he covered himself with and lay down beside her, and put his arms round her again, as close if not more closely still, his head on her pillow, she in the sleeping bag, he beside it. 'Why do you weep?' he whispered. 'Tell me.'

She didn't want to any more, but she couldn't tell him that. 'I don't know. I'm being very stupid,' she murmured.

'You are being a woman. Women weep. I cannot leave you. Do you think I could sleep knowing you are upset?' He laughed softly, teasing, but gently so. 'You do not need to tell me why, it is enough that you are.' He kissed her cheek, then her forehead, but he did not kiss her mouth. And he held her. He would not let her go, not until she was asleep, she knew that. The wild longing she had felt, that had been transmuted into tears, had faded. Something else was there instead; a sense of utter rightness at their being together. He would not attempt to make love to her, she knew that more surely than anything. He sought only to protect her. In that, he proved himself even stronger than she had imagined before, and strangely comforted, she found herself gradually relaxing, the ache soothed away, changed into something far richer and sweeter. And in the moments before she slept, she was aware of the real reason for her tears. They had been for him and his sadness, not for herself.

When morning came it brought the sun, and more—the gradual signs of a thaw. It was a splashing sound which woke Victoria first, a steady drip-drip-drip from outside, and she lay for a moment listening, still in Gregor's arms, and wondered if it meant a rise in temperature—or a burst pipe. It was impossible to remain there any longer. She had to know. She tried to ease herself free, and he stirred, not awake but disturbed, and murmured something she could not hear. 'Gregor,' she whispered. 'Wake up.'

He opened his eyes, and groaned. She doubted he had been comfortable—she thought he would have gone back to his own bed when she fell asleep –she was glad he hadn't. She felt incredibly warm and secure as she looked at his sleepy face, and sighed. 'I'm sorry, Gregor.'

'Why are you so sorry?' he whispered.

'For making you sleep so uncomfortably all night.'

He smiled. 'Is that what you woke me to tell me?'

'No. I can hear water—listen.'

He sat up in an instant, padded to the window and drew back the curtains. She scrambled to her feet and followed him, and he put his arm around her as if if were the most natural thing in the world, and held her to him. 'It is getting warmer,' he exclaimed. 'Come—boots and coats on. We will go outside to see.' He turned, hugged and lifted her, and kissed her soundly, until she gasped for breath. 'The snow is going!'

'Oh. Put me down! You want to go outside *now*?'

'In a few minutes anyway.' He put her down. Of

course he was happy. He had found out all he needed, and in a day or so, he would leave as he intended, and go skiing in Aviemore. And after that, return home to whoever waited. What had she expected? He didn't belong to her, he never would. He was a free spirit, an adventurer, a champion skier whose life style was completely different from her own. She knew she should be feeling a great sense of relief at the thaw, but she wasn't. Knew she should be delighted at the prospect of Uncle Craig coming home—and that was different, of course she looked forward very much to that—but—oh, if only there had been more time. . . .

She went through to the kitchen after visiting the cloakroom under the stairs, and Gregor waited, wellingtons and thick parka on, and Victoria followed suit, and her heart was heavy. They opened the front door, and now there was no doubt. The snow crackled faintly as the warmth touched it, and the air had lost its bite. It was still cold, but less so. He walked to the car and brushed snow off the roof and turned to her. 'In a day, two days, this will be gone,' he told her.

'That's wonderful,' said Victoria. She even managed to look as though she meant it. Gregor gave her a curious glance but said nothing. She followed him to the car.

'Now, let us try and walk round to the back from here,' Gregor went on. 'The exercise and the fresh air will be good for us. You will follow me.' And he turned and led the way, albeit slowly, much, thought Victoria, like someone struggling through porridge. Porridge! We'll have that for breakfast.

'Have you had porridge since you came to Scotland?' she called, and he paused and half turned.

'Porridge? The great national breakfast of this country? No, I have not. Tell me, is it as dreadful as they say?'

'It's wonderful! Well, it would be if we had fresh milk—still—I'll see what I can do.' The air had made her cheeks rosy, it tasted clear and sparkling, like wine. In less than a month it would be Christmas—it was an odd thought for her to have, followed by another. Last Christmas I was with Peter—and I didn't know he was married. And last Christmas I didn't even know of the existence of this man whom I am following, this large dark man who slept beside me last night because I had been crying and he would not leave me. Last Christmas, the world was a poorer place because he wasn't in it, and yet all the time, all through the years leading up till now, we have been related. He has enriched my life although he does not know it, will never know it. She closed her eyes briefly. There were some people who acted as catalysts in the lives of others. Gregor was one such, she knew with an instinct as old as time. He had charisma— he would attract people to him. He was a bright star in the firmament—and she had seen him once, briefly on television, half-forgotten the name but not the impression he had made upon her. He was truly something special.

They were at the back now, in the courtyard, his carved-out path a black line from house to stable, a dark straight path with banked snow on either side. He opened the back door, stamping his wellingtons on the step as he prepared to go in.

Victoria was just about to speak when he caught her arm. 'Wait. Listen,' he said, and looked up. Then she heard it. The distant drone of an engine, coming nearer, nearer.

'A helicopter,' she whispered. 'It's a *helicopter*!'

'Yes. I know.' He walked along his track to the centre of the courtyard and she followed to see, approaching rapidly, a small helicopter. It was making directly for them, just above roof height, nearer and nearer until they could see clearly the number painted on it. The noise was tremendous, the huge rotor blades clicking round at high speed, the machine hovering overhead. 'He is signalling us,' said Gregor, and raising his arms, gave the thumbs up sign. The door opened, an arm came out, waved, and a large piece of paper fluttered down. The helicopter banked and turned, to swoop round above them in a gentle, lazy circular motion as Gregor breasted through the snow to pick up the large sheet of paper which had landed several yards away from them. He read it quickly then looked up as the machine came round. Victoria watched him wave and nod his head vigorously—then the pilot saluted, and the next moment the helicopter soared away. They watched it go, then Gregor came back towards her. He was smiling.

'Gregor, what is it?' she shouted.

'We have work to do,' he said, grinning broadly. 'Much work. We will need lots of porridge first.' He handed her the paper. 'See.'

Printed in block capitals were the words—the *incredible* words:

'UNCLE CRAIG RETURNING HOME BY HELICOPTER

TOMORROW. PLEASE CLEAR AREA OF APPROX. TWELVE FOOT SQUARE, CENTRE OF LAWN AT SIDE OF HOUSE. BEST OF LUCK! JIM ALLEN (PILOT)'

She put her hand to her mouth in delighted amazement. Trust Uncle Craig to do everything in style! She looked at Gregor, her eyes shining. 'He's coming home! We can tell him!'

'You are very pleased? So am I, Victoria. Come, let us go in now.' He put his arm round her shoulder. He did it as though it was the most natural thing in the world, and she thought, I wish he wouldn't. I could get to like it—correction—I already like it—and I'll miss it when he's gone. She looked up at him as they went in, along the dark passage to the kitchen—and just before they reached the kitchen door, Gregor stopped, turned, put his arms round her, and kissed her full on her lips. It was a lovely kiss; it was warm, and sensual, and it made her tremble and go dizzy, and when she recovered her voice, she said.

'Why did you do that?'

'Because I am happy. Are you not?'

'Of course.' He regards me like a *sister*, she thought. A *younger* sister. And why the hell shouldn't he? He's at least thirteen years older than me, we're sort of cousins—he's got *thousands* of gorgeous super-sophisticated women falling at his feet and I look like a teenage boy dressed in my sweater and jeans with no make-up on, and oh *hell*—after today it will all be different—so I've got nothing to lose—I'm not a teenage boy, I don't need to look like one, I'm a woman, and this evening, he is going to *see* me as one. Just one evening, but I'll make it one to remember, for him and for me. And he'll look at me differently, I'll see to that. Oh, yes, oh yes indeedy. Sure, I love him, but it's not the end of the world. 'Of course I'm happy,' she repeated, and she laughed, and went on into the kitchen. 'I'll make porridge, and then we'll find a couple of spades.' And later on I'm going to wash my hair, look out my make-up, and find something just a little bit different to wear, but you're not going to find that out until this evening, my darling. And she looked across the kitchen at him as she hopped on one leg removing her wellingtons. The words of an old song came into her mind. 'I'll give you something to remember me by,' and she smiled to herself, and bent her head to pull up her socks so that he wouldn't see.

The thaw was very gradual, but there. They listened to the radio news at ten o'clock, after breakfasting on porridge and coffee, and had it confirmed. Snow ploughs were gradually clearing major roads; the worst was over. It made their task slightly easier, but not much. They worked for two hours before lunch, and again afterwards until at nearly four o'clock they were both able to down spades and survey the results of their work with satisfaction. A large circle had been cleared, more than was asked in the note, and from it lay a narrow path leading to the back door, which was the nearer. Victoria was roasting, so too was Gregor who had already taken off his parka and whose forehead shone with sweat. He looked around him. 'You did well, Victoria,' he said. 'I think we can celebrate with a drink.'

'A good idea,' she agreed. 'Uncle Craig has laid some very good champagne in the cellars. I think a drop now wouldn't come amiss.' She picked up her fallen shovel and turned to go in. Her back ached, her legs ached, but above all, her arms were like lead. Oh for a bath, she thought. But that little pleasure would have to wait a day or two. There was other work to be done first.

They sat by the fire in the drawing room and sipped ice-cold champagne, and it was lovely. 'What shall we have for dinner tonight?' she asked him.

'What would you like?'

'More to the point—what have we *got*?'

He smiled. 'There is some fish in the freezer that should be eaten without much delay——'

'Then fish it will be. We'll eat in here tonight I think, by a good log fire, and——' she refilled their glasses, 'we'll have another bottle of this excellent champagne,' and as a slight flicker of dismay touched his face, she added: 'Don't worry. It's only sherry that has an unfortunate effect on me. I shan't touch that again in a hurry—champagne's lovely though, I can drink it for ever. Well, nearly.'

He raised his glass. 'It is indeed a fine champagne. And, yes we will eat in here.'

'I need to wash my hair before we eat. I've not done it for days.'

'There is plenty of time, Victoria. You have no more work to do today. You have done enough.'

She laughed. 'You did more digging than I did!'

'I am stronger.' He shrugged. 'It is natural that I should.' Oh how I love you, she thought. When you shrug, or smile, or just look at me. Everything you do in fact is something special because you *are* something special, and I wonder if you know it?

Perhaps special people never did know, not consciously. Perhaps only deep down inside were they aware of it and what drew others to them. Thank you, God, for letting me know him, she said, a simple, direct prayer of gratitude. She looked down at her glass in which tiny bubbles rose in straight lines. I shall think of you whenever I drink champagne in future, and make a silent toast to you wherever you are, she thought. Wherever you are. . . .

She rose to her feet. 'If you'll give me twenty minutes in the kitchen to wash my hair, then I'll tidy up in here and set a table for us.' She leaned over and poured more champagne in his glass. 'Finish the bottle. Would you like one of your cigars?'

'An excellent idea, thank you.' His eyes followed her—she was aware of them on her back as she moved—and she lit a paper spill and held it to the cigar for him, and went out. While her hair dried in the warm room she would tidy it, and then, when he prepared the meal she would go up and change and make-up. Her thoughts were pleasant, anticipatory. I could never in a million years be a femme fatale, she thought, as she went upstairs for her shampoo and dressing-gown but I'm not a plain Jane either. And just for once, if only for a few minutes, he's going to look at me and see me not as a young cousin ten times removed, but as a woman. And she smiled to herself.

The table was laid and in place by the fire, and Victoria had brought in two dining chairs and set the candelabra in the centre of the table. She would light the candles just before he came in with the dinner. She looked around her and was satisfied that all that could be done had been done. It was time for the transformation scene. She picked up the lamp, and carried it along the corridor and up the stairs. Ghostly shadows rose and fell as the lamp bobbed with her steps. Echoes of the past, when there was no electricity, surrounded her. She had never been frightened, would never be frightened, in this house. If there were ghosts, they were friendly ones. Thus had her namesake walked along the corridors, lamp or candle held high, dressed though in long gowns, not jeans—and Victoria halted her step at that thought. Long gown—*long* sweeping-the-floor-gown. Of course! Of *course*. In one of the chests in one of the attics, there had been several very old, very faded, but very beautiful dresses. She and her sister had tried them on as children, she had seen them during their search for books so recently but not given them a thought. Of course none might fit—that was, alas, eminently possible. But to look would only take a few minutes. She turned and went up the attic stairs, more slowly, for they were steep, reached the top, turned, knew exactly where the dresses were. It was still very cold up there and she shivered, but she wasn't going down until she had looked. She put the lamp on a chest of drawers and opened a cedarwood chest. The faintest whisper of lavender came out as she lifted first one then another dress out, tried them against her, put them down. Too small, too short—but then, ah then, she lifted out one that had been carefully wrapped in silver paper and held it against her, and it was long enough. And she put the waist of it to her waist, and it was large enough. It was of a delicate pink silk, the material all hand sewn, with tiny mother-of-pearl buttons down the back, and sloping shoulders and a deep rounded neck. The sleeves were long and full going into a band at the wrists, the bodice sloping gently in to the waist, the skirt full, with tiny flounces at the hem. She put the material to her face and it was smooth and cool. This was the one she would try on. If it didn't fit, never mind, but if it did, ah then! Wrapped with it was a large, beautifully coloured shawl in fine Indian wool. They belonged together.

She closed the trunk and carried the dress and shawl down to her bedroom and took off her dressing-gown. Holding the dress up, she estimated the minimum number of buttons she needed to undo to get into it, and unfastened them, her fingers clumsy with the cold. Then taking a deep breath and holding her stomach in, she slipped the dress over her head. Down, down, down, it went, silky smooth, cold, so cold, as yet, and it was on. She'd *done* it. Victoria was slim, and she must have lost a few pounds in the last few days—and the dress might have been made for her. She reached up and back and fastened the tiny buttons. Oh for zips! Then, it was done and she put on the shawl as well and she held the lamp high and walked slowly—impossible to move quickly as yet in the unfamiliar skirt—towards the mirror.

It was like seeing a ghost, seeing herself for the first time dressed thus and a faint shiver of recognition ran through her. It was as if she were looking at an image from the past. It could not be possible that this dress and shawl had been worn by that other Victoria—or could it? Just for a fleeting moment it seemed so. She turned, and the image turned. She held the skirt out, and it swished silkily, rustling. She let it fall, and from somewhere seemed to hear a faint echo. . . .

Victoria went to the dressing table and sat down, putting her dressing-gown over her shoulders to warm her and protect the dress. Then she began to make-up. She had finished and was about to comb her hair when she heard Gregor's voice calling her.

'I'll be down in two minutes,' she answered as, on impulse, she swept her hair back and up, and looked at her reflection. Could she do it? Did she know *how* to do it? She had always worn her hair in casual style either loose or tied back with a ribbon when working, but now, on an irresistible impulse, she searched for, and found in the drawer, several old side combs and pins that had been there for years, ever since dressing-up days. It was so easy, now that she was determined. She twisted her hair back, then up, secured it firmly with combs and pins, and gazed at herself, resisting an impish grin. She looked totally different! She pulled out her tongue and her reflection did the same. Yes, it's me she thought. This was it. Time for the grand entrance. Please, oh please, don't let me fall over and go sprawling and spoil everything, she thought, and it made her laugh.

Picking up the lamp with one hand, gathering her skirts and trailing shawl ends up with the other, she began to walk towards the door. Along the corridor, down the stairs—very slowly—along the bottom corridor, the skirt rustling as she went. She wore no shoes, only tights, and her feet were whisper quiet, and the door to the drawing room was ajar, and she could hear the chink of glass against bottle, so Gregor was waiting for her. Good.

Then—inside. And she paused just inside the doorway, and Gregor looked up. Looked up—and saw her. She saw the shock on his face, saw it so clearly in the light from the candles he had lit. Saw him rise slowly to his feet, the glass in his hand crashing to the carpet, spilling, not breaking. She saw his face, and she had never seen him look like that before and for a second she was frightened, and said: 'Gregor—what is it?' and began to walk towards him, silently gliding across the space between them, lamp held high.

'*Mon dieu*——' he said. 'My God—it is you, Victoria.' He bent to pick up the fallen glass as she reached him, and she saw that he had gone white. She put the lamp down on the table.

'What is it?' she said. 'What is *wrong*?' She hadn't intended this. Not this.

'For a moment,' he answered, 'I thought it was Victoria—the other Victoria. For a moment, as you walked in, I thought I was seeing a ghost. That dress and shawl you are wearing—they are the same as in my picture.'

CHAPTER NINE

'IT is incredible,' said Gregor his voice husky, little more than a whisper. 'Please—turn round.'

Victoria turned slowly, her head held high, the elegance of the outfit making her feel so different, so—graceful, somehow. It was difficult for her to think that only a few hours previously she had been wielding a nifty spade, digging a helicopter landing pad out of snow. She stood in profile to him. She had made her entrance all right—with more effect than she could have imagined. He was still stunned, she could tell. His eyes showed it. He had not once taken them off her since she had entered the room. It was as if she had caught him off balance. He looked as though he had been knocked out, and was recovering.

'You mean, these could have been Victoria's?' she asked, disbelievingly.

'I think so,' he said. 'My heart stopped when you came in. I thought I was seeing her.'

'And were you frightened?' She turned now to face him, smiling.

'No.' He shook his head, then moved towards her. 'I cannot put into words what I felt—it was—like seeing a picture come to life—it is too difficult to explain——'

'No—it's not,' she said softly, and looked up at him. 'For I understand exactly. It happened to me, here in this room when you walked in for the first time and I looked round thinking you were my

uncle. I thought then, for a moment, that—it—
you—were like a medieval picture come to life—
for a second, my heart stopped too.' She paused.
'Oh yes—I understand very well.'

He reached out to touch the smooth silk of the
shoulder of her dress. 'So beautiful,' he said. 'So
very beautiful.' But his eyes were on her face, not
on the dress, and the hand he touched her with
was not perfectly steady, nor was his voice, and
she thought, yes, he's seeing me as a woman, but
it's not exactly what I want, not this way. I want
him to see *me*, not some image he's carried around
with him, and she moved slightly away.

'We'd better eat now, hadn't we?' she asked.

'Yes. Of course. It is ready.' He too had gone to
trouble. The fish was perfectly poached in a
delicate sauce, and with it he had done vegetables,
and there was the last of the fruit to follow. They
talked as they ate, but of her uncle, of how he
would be on his arrival, and the meal was a
pleasant time, but the atmosphere was different
from anything that had gone before. Gregor was
different. And when the meal was over, he would
not let her help him clear away, or make coffee,
and she smiled to herself, and thought, well, I
certainly gave him something to remember me by,
and she sat back on the settee by the fire after he
had moved the table away, and sipped her
champagne. She ached all over after the spadework
she had done. I only hope I can get out of this
dress when it's bedtime, she thought. This was
their last evening alone. She lifted her glass so that
the firelight came through it and it shone ruby red
and gold. The room was warm, the air with the
faintest scent of lavender in it and the candles he

had placed on the mantelpiece flickered in a slight draught as the door opened and Gregor returned bearing the tray with coffee and liqueurs. He sat down beside her and put the tray on one of the footstools. A strand of Victoria's hair had come loose, and she caught it back and tucked it into a comb. And quite suddenly the atmosphere was changed, so tense that she caught her breath. He handed her a cup of coffee, his eyes darker, more shadowed in the dim light. There were no lamps lit, only the candles. The air was almost misty.

'Will you decide to live here?' he asked, and she nodded.

'I'll have to talk it over with my uncle, of course—but—this is where my heart is, where it has always been. I have many friends up here, nearly as many as in London.'

'Yes?'

'People I've known from childhood. I would have phoned a few, but——' She looked over towards the phone and grimaced. 'Never mind, it will soon be mended, I'm sure, as will the power.'

'So you will not find it lonely?'

What an odd word to use. 'I'm never lonely,' she replied truthfully. 'I may be alone sometimes, but I never feel lonely. Do you?'

He smiled. 'No. I too am the same. There are many times when I have gone away to the mountains, and slept alone in some ski hut—to wake up and see the dawn when you are several thousand feet up is something beyond description. I could not put it into words, Victoria.'

'There are mountains round here. I've only walked up—the easier hills really—in daylight of course. Perhaps I'm not as adventurous as you,

Gregor—but even then, there is something magical about being so high above the world.'

She looked directly at him at the same moment he looked at her, and she trembled inwardly, her body warm with a heat that did not come from any fire. The fire was inside her.

He cleared his throat. 'Tonight it will be possible for us to return to our bedrooms,' he said. 'I have been up——'

'Yes. It's not as cold.' She stroked the cup of hot coffee reflectively. 'It will be more—comfortable.'

'Yes.' He seemed as if about to add something—and changed his mind. A silence grew, a silence so *loud* that it was almost more than she could bear. What is happening? she thought. Her heart was beating rapidly, uncomfortably so. He was beside her, only a foot or so away, yet it was as if they touched. Desperately, quickly, to break that unbearable tension she said:

'Do you have parties at Christmas?' A banal, *stupid* question, but she could think of no other.

'It is a busy time at the hotel. I stay there and help my parents.' He paused. 'And you, Victoria? Do you?'

'Yes. I'd like to spend this Christmas up here—with my family if possible. We did it a couple of years ago, my brother and his fiancée, my sister and her husband, and we had a party that went on for two whole days.' She laughed. 'It was wonderful. Uncle Craig loves giving parties——'

'And this house must have seen many, over the years.'

'Yes.' It was easier to keep talking than to allow silence to fall. Much easier, especially if it were on this light level. 'We put fairy lights in the hall, and outside, along the porch, and cars lined the drive, and my brother ran a mobile disco, and my father and sister's husband acted as barmen, and when the drink ran out someone went out for more—I'd forgotten that!' she smiled at him, and a shiver ran down her spine at the look in his eyes, and her voice faltered. 'We—Uncle Craig w-went down and fetched up a case of wine, and—I remember now, the police called in—and left the lights on in their squad car so that the batteries went flat—and we had to go out and give them a push.'

'The police?'

'Oh, it's all right. They often call, this house being so remote. They're always sure of a drink when they come here, especially round Christmas.' He smiled at that.

'I see. And they had a few drinks that night?'

'We had to sober them up with black coffee before we let them go!'

'You will not miss London and its bright lights then, will you, when you come?'

'No. Would you miss the bright lights of Paris, if you left there?'

'No.' He poured two liqueurs out with a steady hand. 'It is my home—but yet it is not my home, you understand.'

Yes, she understood, and remembered her tears for him. 'I know,' she said quietly.

'Yes, I think you do—more than anybody.' More than your woman who waits for you, she wondered, but did not say. She picked up the glass with the Benedictine in and sipped it. Her head was a little light with the champagne, but pleasantly so. She winced as she put the glass down, aching muscles protesting and he said:

'What is the matter?'

'I'm not used to doing a lot of digging—my body is letting me know. I ache in places where I didn't even know I'd got muscles!'

'Poor Victoria,' but the words hid a smile.

'It's all right for *you*,' she protested.

'Yes, and I am sorry. But I do not think you would have allowed me to do everything on my own, would you?'

'Of course not. I wonder what time he'll arrive?'

'No earlier than ten, I should think.'

'Yes, you're probably right. The doctor would want to see him before he left.' She looked at her watch, holding it at an angle to catch the light on its face. 'It's nearly nine-thirty, Gregor. I'd like an early night I think.' Because it is difficult to sit here with you and I'm not sure why, she thought, and touched his hand lightly. 'You won't mind, will you?'

'No, of course not.' She finished the liqueur in her glass.

'I'll be up early in the morning and get everything ready for Uncle Craig.' She rose to her feet, and Gregor too stood. 'I'll fill two bottles— one for you, shall I?'

'No. Not in that dress. I will do that, Victoria, for you. If you wish to go now, I shall bring yours up as soon as it is ready.'

'Thank you.' She lifted her skirt slightly to enable her to move and picked up a candle, and he went over towards the door and held it open, an old-fashioned gesture that in no way seemed out of place, dressed as she was.

'And—thank you, for wearing that beautiful gown.'

'It was a pleasure.' She floated along the corridor, candle held aloft, and up the stairs. Candle safely in holder on her bedside table, shawl on chair, she lifted her arms to undo the buttons— and couldn't. She tried again, and with a great effort managed the first one, and sat down on the bed, biting her lip. There was one obvious and simple solution—to ask Gregor. She was frightened of damaging the delicate material if she struggled any more, and it was a struggle, no doubt about that. She marvelled that she had actually managed to fasten any of the buttons now, but she would not have missed that experience for anything in the world. And the thought came unbidden into her mind—he will remember that as long as he lives, and so shall I.

While she waited, because it was impossible to sit still, she went to the bathroom, and on returning, creamed off her make-up and loosed her hair, which tumbled down her back, long and free. She saw the light that flickered outside the doorway, turned to face him as he entered, and said: 'Gregor, will you help me unfasten these buttons? I'm afraid I can't manage.'

He put the hot water bottle inside her bed, placed his lamp on her bedside table next to the candle, and turned to her. 'If you wish, of course,' he answered, and she went towards him, and it was dark with the shadows all around them, only that pool of light that didn't reach the further corners of the room, and she turned her back to him, and felt his hands at her neck, felt his body behind her, was so powerfully aware of him that it was an effort to breathe. He moved her hair aside, and his fingers were a caress, strong and yet so gentle, tingling where they touched her skin, leaving fire in their wake. And she stood perfectly still, with what great effort he could not know, and felt the loosening as he undid the buttons one by one. 'Was it because your arms were stiff?' his voice came from near to her ear, a whisper, no more.

'Yes.'

'I have a cream for muscular pains. It is in my room. I carry it everywhere with me—especially when I intend to ski.'

'Do you? Thank you.' She had to clear her throat before she could even swallow.

The buttons were done now, not only the few she had needed, but all of them. 'Get into bed. I will rub your arms for you.'

'No——' but he did not hear. He had gone. Victoria eased the dress off downwards—no way she could lift it over her head now—and, shivering, climbed into bed. She wore bra and pants and tights, that was all.

'Lie on your stomach,' his voice came from the door, and she turned, obediently and lay flat, arms beside her and thought—does he *know* what he's doing?

The next moment, coldness at the top of both arms, then pressure as he rubbed in the cream. She had expected sharp-smelling liniment, but this had an almost sweet scent to it. And oh, the touch of him, the wonderful, wonderful touch of his fingers on her arms, and on her back, as impersonal as a doctor's, yet so warm and strong.

'Is that better?'

'Yes—it's marvellous—I——' he had stopped, abruptly. She turned. 'Have you finished?' He sat there, looking at her, and her heart pounded—and then she knew why.

'It is better I stop now, I think,' he said, and his voice was unsteady. She lay there looking up at him and her love for him shone in her eyes, and was in her voice as she whispered:

'Yes. I know.'

'I think not.' But he did not move away. Instead he reached out and stroked her hair. The sweet scent was on his fingers and she said:

'What is it?' her heart pounding so much it would burst if it went on any longer. Her head pounded as well, so much it was as if he could hear. Light danced; her eyes were playing her tricks, it was as if he moved, but he wasn't. He was sitting there just looking at her, his hand on her hair, and in the air around them, a shimmering stillness, a waiting. Then, and she had known it was what he would do next, it had a sense of inevitability about it; his head came down, blotting out what little light there was, and his mouth came down on hers, and he took her in his arms, sliding his hands beneath her back, raising her to meet his lips, tasting their sweetness, the sweetness of all the ages—it was a kiss like no other there had ever been before. A kiss of such absolute perfection she thought she would die, thought her heart would burst. There was no sense of time, no sense of anything save the explosion within, the urgency of that moment, the need.

She clung helplessly to him, her own urgent responses on fire in an instant, her whole body blazing in the sudden heat of devastating awareness of that which they had both known was inevitable from the moment they had met. She had been waiting for this moment all her life. Everything that had ever happened had only been leading to this. There was only the here, and the now, no one else existed; in all the world, just the two of them, together in that room from which there was no escape. Skin touched, breath mingled, heat blazed wilder than all the fires that had ever burnt, and the room rocked with the force of passion that had been ignited with one simple touch.

Cloth softly moving, hands urgently discarding, no more barriers between them, both inside between warm sheets, limbs entangling, hard against soft, muscular against weak, fingers seeking, finding, no words needed, none spoken.

She gasped, long low and shuddering as his mouth explored her skin, his tongue touched, gentled, delighted with its sweetness against her breast, his hands roved above, below, between. . . .

She had never known, had never imagined, eyes closed, blind with desire, she took and held him, that hardness against her, into her, and movement was a mounting crescendo of sounds and feeling and deep, deep awareness that took her with a force such as she had not thought anyone capable. There was no coherent thought, the primitive urgency went far and beyond any reason. There was a wonder and an ecstasy about, the dizzying pinnacles of the mountain top, the swift plunge downwards and again, and again swifter, then slowing in a strange rhythmic pattern all its own. She saw stars, she saw worlds beyond worlds that were endless. She was completely lost. Both were.

There was hair beneath her convulsively clutching hands, his head, raising now, watching her, both eyes opened, she seeing the wildness in him, his nostrils flaring, mouth stretched as if in agony—but it was not agony they knew it, it was a shared ecstasy, their bodies damp yet burning, their every movement co-ordinated to a fine perfection, a deep pulsing rhythm that went on for ever and ever. . . . Until, then, great gasps, a harsh cry from Gregor, her own response, faster now, faster, she would die, she would die—aaah—oh, no, oh no—please aah——

And then they lay still, spent with the force of that mutual, incredible passion, and she curled into his arms with a deep, deep sigh, and tumbled into immediate sleep in which there were no dreams, but the vivid images and memories of a lovemaking so perfect that nothing else can ever happen again in life that would match it.

She woke, raising herself slightly, and her body ached all over, every inch of it, and she marvelled that she had slept at all. At last, she knew. She was a woman, complete and fulfilled. Gregor lay beside her, and opened his eyes. The light that came in through the window was thin and watery, pre-dawn light. She shivered and snuggled closer to him, and thought, I love you so much, if I never make love again, I will have this one perfect time to remember for ever and ever. He turned and stroked her hair, smiling sleepily, his eyes shadowed and mysterious in the early morning greyness.

'You are so wonderful,' he murmured.

'So were you,' she whispered, and, teasing,

moved her leg across him—and was startled by the instant response. 'Oh,' she said. He reached down to her breasts, touching, stroking lightly.

'Oh,' he said, with the same inflexion in his voice.

'Oh yes,' she answered. 'Oh—yes——'

He moved. There was not the same urgency now, more a languorous, half-sleeping yet waking response, his mouth softened by sleep, his lips incredibly gentle, as teasing as she had been a moment previously, his fingers slower, knowing exactly now where to go, his body wakening only gradually to that greater response needed. Snuggling beneath the sheets where the air was warm, all was gentler, more slowly paced, each knowing the other and what pleasured, each knowing too that there was all the time in the world, there were hours before they needed to leave the bed. Flesh was warm and soft with sleep, hands guided, responded, Victoria leaned over him and kissed him full on the mouth, then slid over him, and lay on top of him, giving herself to him, ah, so different now, so different, and—ah—that was good. 'Oh yes,' she murmured again, but this time with a different meaning, 'ah—there—yes—there——'

They stood outside, coats and wellingtons on, and Gregor looked down at her and smiled softly, almost gently. 'Are you well now?'

She felt the colour rush to her skin. The helicopter could be heard distantly. They had been keeping a watch, going out every few minutes since breakfast to listen, and now, it was nearly here. Their time together, alone, was nearly over. And just as well, she thought wryly, or I might have been tempted. . . .

His life was not hers. For whatever reason he had made love to her, and she thought she knew, deep down—good old-fashioned lust and the extreme availability built in to their situation—he had his life away from here, and she had hers. Like ships that pass in the night she thought inconsequentially. Cousins, and yet not, the relationship remote, a tenuous link—the act purely physical on his part, she knew that. She was not so naive as to suppose he had fallen in love with her. He was a charming man, with impeccable manners—and he had a woman waiting patiently for his return. Perhaps he was already regretting his passion. If so, he hid it well. His manner to her since before breakfast had been warm and caring. Now, he had his arm around her, holding her to him in the crisp clean air as they waited.

'Yes. I'm fine. And you?' She made sure that nothing showed in her eyes. Her spirit was too fiercely independent to allow her to do that. What had happened was over, would not happen again.

'Very well thank you.' His tone was grave, only the merest hint of laughter lurking there.

'He's here. Nearly—oh—look.' The helicopter circled round, lower and lower, and all other thoughts were washed from her mind as she watched, heart in mouth at the precision of that huge machine. She could see a face at the window, and waved, and received one in return. The kettle was on, food waited, in case he was hungry. Lower still, then a gentle drop, right in the centre of their circle, and a tall man dressed in dark overalls leapt to the ground as the rotor blades clicked to a halt and dashed round to the other side to open the passenger door. Victoria ran forward laughing as the young pilot helped Uncle Craig out. Then she was hugging him, crying and laughing all at the same time as Gregor shook the pilot's hand, appeared to be thanking him.

The next minute they were in the kitchen and Uncle Craig, looking very well, was sitting in a chair introducing the tall, cheerful-faced young man as Jim Allen and asking him if he would like a drink.

Jim Allen looked longingly at the boiling kettle. 'Well,' he drawled, in an unmistakably American accent, 'I guess they can spare me for an extra ten minutes back at the base. Thanks, I will.'

'Do sit down Mr Allen,' Victoria said. 'Tea or coffee?'

'Black coffee, two sugars ma'am please,' he settled down in a chair and while Gregor fetched beakers Victoria brewed tea for her uncle. 'Say—nearly forgot, Mr Mitchell. Your things! I'll go and get them.'

'I brought some food with me,' Uncle Craig explained, seeing Victoria's puzzlement. 'And the post. There's a couple of letters for you.'

As Jim Allen stood, Gregor said, 'I will come and help you,' and followed him out.

'A couple of letters for me?' echoed Victoria. 'How?'

'Simple. When I got to hospital I asked them to see about redirecting my mail—I was expecting a parcel of interesting stamps from a friend in Nottingham. So, yesterday when they arrived, they also delivered the two for you.'

'I see.' She smiled. 'You're looking extremely well.'

'And so I am. A little groggy on my feet but it's good to be home.'

'You know the phones were out of order, or I'd have called you. Gregor and I have so much to tell you—but it can wait till later. It's too good to rush.'

Her uncle chuckled. 'Sounds intriguing—but I won't ask.' She hugged him, gave him a kiss on his forehead and said:

'Oh, I'm so glad you're home.'

'And how have you been getting on with Gregor, eh? Bit of a facer that, being stranded here with a stranger?'

'We've got on fine,' she answered brightly. 'He's the ideal one to be stranded with. You never told me he was a skiing champion!'

Craig's eyebrows shot up. 'Good God, is he? I never knew that——'

The two men arrived back carrying cartons and a suitcase, stamping their feet. They put the boxes down and Gregor lifted out a parcel which he put on the table, and two letters which he handed to Victoria with the words:

'These are for you, Victoria.' There was something odd about his expression.

'Thank you.' She took them. The top one was from her mother. She looked at the second one and shock caused her heart to leap. Quietly she put them down on the working surface and went to pour out the tea. She was aware of Gregor's eyes upon her but there was nothing she could do about it. Not now, not with everyone there. The unmistakably familiar writing on the second letter was Peter's. And somehow, Gregor knew.

CHAPTER TEN

UNCLE CRAIG was seated in the drawing room with a cigar in one hand and a small glass of his best port in the other. Comfortable, feet up on the footstool, with a blazing log fire to gaze at, he was a happy man. Victoria left them talking and went out to the kitchen to prepare lunch and unpack the food he had brought.

The letters waited for her, and she opened her mother's first and read that. A letter full of gossip, expressing concern about the snow, but sure that Victoria would manage, and would she please phone when she could? She put the letter down with a smile which disappeared as she picked up Peter's. Turning the envelope over, she knew how Gregor had known. Peter's name and address were on the back. She slit it open with a knife, feeling a coldness within her as she did so. She didn't want to read it but she was going to. Whatever he did or said now could hold no interest for her, she was completely free of him, and when she returned to London she would write and tell him so. For he was getting a divorce, he said, and he still loved her and wanted to see her. She felt nothing as she read the words, not even a sadness that he hadn't been honest with her before. She put the letter down next to her mother's on the working top and went to unpack the groceries and vegetables.

And Gregor's voice came from the doorway. 'I have come to make a cup of tea for your uncle.'

'Fine. The kettle's just boiled.' She was absorbed in her task, and didn't see his eyes go to the letter. 'Oh, look, a cauliflower! A *fresh* cauliflower and carrots——' she looked up, smiling, and Gregor wasn't smiling back at her, not at all. His eyes were hard. 'What is it?' she asked in a quiet voice.

'You have read your letters?'

'Yes. One from my mother, the other——' she hesitated, 'from Peter.'

'So I guessed. So—that will be someone else waiting for you in London?'

Victoria was puzzled. Did he think—'Just a minute! What are you getting at?' She went over and picked it up and handed it to him. 'Read it if you're so interested. He's getting a divorce—and he wants to see me. Only *I don't want to see him.*'

'I do not read other people's letters.' He had changed, face hard, unlike anything she had seen before.

'Suit yourself.' She shrugged and turned away, crumpled the letter up and flung it in the bin under the sink. He was angry when he had no reason to be. 'I'm going to get lunch. I'll bring in that tea. You can go back now, Gregor.' She didn't particularly want to talk to him while he was in this mood. Whatever had brought it on—and it surely couldn't just be Peter's letter—she had too much to do, too much else to think about. He was disturbing her by his very presence, and she didn't want an argument. In a way Peter's letter had disturbed her as well and she needed time to get it out of her system. She would have preferred to burn it, to erase it completely, and would do so later—but not when he was there. She turned and he was still standing there.

'You were still in love with him when you came here,' he said.

'And I'm not now,' she retorted. Oh lord, couldn't he guess *why*?

'It does not happen that fast.'

She felt her own temper rising, battered by the inexplicable waves of anger coming from him, and snapped: 'Well, I'm sure *you're* the expert on matters of the heart! You must have had enough experience—oh no—I forgot! Silly me! You've never loved *any* woman, have you?' Eyes blazing, she faced him, their eyes locked, neither looking away. 'It's just sex with you, isn't it? So you wouldn't know how fast anyone can fall *out* of love because *you've* never been *in* it!' She whirled away again, banged a tin of peas down on the table—and he walked out without another word His face was white. Stricken, Victoria gazed after him, totally numbed by what had happened. It was quite inexplicable. She had to rest her hands on the table, breathing fast, for a few seconds. Then, slowly, she went over to the stove and lit the gas under the kettle again to make her uncle's tea.

She had been so looking forward to telling him the news, with Gregor, about their discoveries. They had agreed, before the helicopter arrived, to wait until after lunch when the tale could be told properly, but now some of the joy had gone out of the prospect. There was a bitter taste in her mouth as she saw again that bleak, hard look in Gregor's eyes. Never before had he looked at her like that, not even when she had first arrived—perhaps, she thought, that was how he was with women—afterwards. 'Oh God.' She put her hand to her mouth. He regarded her as little more than a tramp—she turned in anguish, unseeing—caught her hand on the kettle and knocked it flying. Boiling water gushed over her hand and she screamed in pain and instinctively dashed to the sink and plunged it into the bowl of cold water that waited for the vegetables to be washed.

Waves of pain washed over her. Gasping for breath she stood there, fighting nausea. She must not panic, or faint, she must not. It would be all right in a minute—she had to tell them. She walked unsteadily away, towards the door, holding her hand away from her, biting her lip to stop herself from crying out. She would not cry, she *would not*.

It was the longest walk of her life and she reached the door of the drawing room, and opened it. Uncle Craig looked round. Gregor did not. He was intent on a book. 'I've—I'm afraid I've scalded my hand,' she began. 'Uncle Craig—please——' The room was going round but she held tight to the door handle as she saw Gregor look up, stand, walk quickly towards her. He caught her as she fell. She heard his muttered exclamation, and wondered if she had managed to annoy him further, but it no longer seemed to matter. It was all fading away, all pain, all feeling, all thought. . . .

She was lying on the settee when she came round to the pungent sting of ammonia in her nostrils, and pushed the smelling salts feebly away. Gregor knelt beside her. His face was white, and she thought bemusedly, oh, he's still angry—then he spoke. 'Victoria—I am going to put ointment on your hand, and then a bandage.'

'The kettle—I knocked the kettle—you must go

and check the gas,' she said, fearful lest the water had put out the flames, fearful only of that.

Uncle Craig's voice came, soothing from behind the settee, and she looked up. 'I'll go and see, my darling. Just you stay there and let Gregor look after you.' She managed a faint smile at his concerned face.

'I'm all right. It was just—the pain—I'm sorry I fainted. That was silly of——'

'Ssh——' the old man leaned over. 'Don't talk. Just get well.' He went slowly away and Victoria was left alone with Gregor. She stared at him.

'I'll manage,' she said. 'Please don't trouble yourself——'

'Don't be stupid,' he answered. 'I have trained in first aid——'

'Well you would have, wouldn't you?' He was holding her arm, quite gently. Her hand hurt like hell, as if a thousand wasps had stung it, but she wasn't going to let him see that. 'I'm all right——'

'Did you put your hand in cold water?' He was ignoring her, examining the pink skin so tightly stretched across the back of it.

'Yes. I'm not entirely stupid you know. If you pass me the cream——' She faltered as he looked at her, and went silent. There was such intensity in his eyes, such a whiteness round his mouth. Anger? It was impossible to tell. She only knew she dare say no more. He squeezed out a large amount of ointment on to a wad of gauze, spread it, then laid it with infinite care across the back of her hand. It was cold, and for a few moments the pain was obliterated, only to return. Her hand now throbbed. He bandaged it skilfully and had just finished when her uncle returned.

'Can she have a drink of tea?' he asked Gregor, who nodded.

'Yes. With sugar, and two aspirin.' He looked up at the older man's concerned face. 'She will be all right in an hour or two. She put her hand in cold water immediately and that helped to reduce the blistering.' He was talking about her as if she wasn't there. Craig nodded.

'Thank the lord. How did it happen?'

'I was going to make your tea—I put out my hand and it must have h-hit the kettle.' She bit her lip. 'Stupid——'

'Never mind. Accidents will happen. Look at me!' He smiled and came round to her. 'Don't worry. If Gregor says you'll be all right, then you will. I'll go and make that tea for you.'

'No, sir. I will. Please sit down.' Gregor packed everything away in the first aid box and rose to his feet. Silently he went out and Uncle Craig sat down wearily, as if the effort had tired him. Victoria needed to reassure him.

'I'm fine now, honestly. Oh! I was going to do lunch——'

'Tsk! We'll manage. You know me. If there's nothing, cheese and biscuits—incidentally I brought a lovely wedge of cheese home, cheddar. One of the nurses went and did all the shopping for me this morning—lovely girl—so it's all fresh stuff. The village was just getting back to normal when I left—I was worried about you, my love. But you managed all right, hey?'

'Perfectly.' She smiled at him, and Gregor returned. He sat on the footstool beside her and gave her two aspirins.

'Take those, and drink this slowly, Victoria.' He

handed her a beaker of tea.

'Thank you,' she said, eyes on him. 'And thank you for your efficient first aid.'

'Do you feel better?'

'Much better.' I'm only sorry I made such a fool of myself last night—and this morning. Still, with any luck, you'll think *you* were one of many as well, instead of the first. 'Thank you,' she added. He would never touch her again. Never. Except perhaps to bandage her hand, and if she could do that herself, she would. The unspoken words were in her eyes for only him to see. She wished he would move away, and a moment later, he did. Perhaps, after all, he could read her thoughts.

'If you will excuse me, I will prepare lunch.' He smiled at Uncle Craig. 'It is a pleasure to have fresh vegetables.' Victoria sipped the hot over-sweet tea and watched him. How different he was with her uncle. How very different from that white-faced man she had confronted in the kitchen.

'Need any help?' the older man enquired.

'No thank you.' He went as silently as before, and Craig looked at her.

'He is a lovely man, isn't he? Just like his father.' He shook his head. 'I can't tell you how happy I am that he came.'

'Yes. Lovely.' She closed her eyes. 'You don't mind if I do this, do you? It's knocked me a bit——'

'Of course. I shall just sit and read while you rest, my dear.'

'There is something I'd like to talk to you about though. It's something I've been thinking about for a while,' she said. 'I've always felt that this was my home, as you know—always had an affinity for Drummell—how would you feel if I said I'd like to live here?'

For a moment she thought he hadn't heard, and opened her eyes in alarm, to see him sitting looking at her, mouth open, tears in his eyes.

'Live here?' he whispered. 'Oh, Victoria! You're not just saying that, are you? You *mean* it?' His voice had gone husky, and she sat up and held out her good hand—her left one—to him.

'Of course I mean it! I love you, and I love here——' he reached over and held her hand.

'You'd make me the happiest man in the world. I've always known you belonged here. More than Anne or Michael—both of whom I love as dearly as you—more than them, or anyone, this is your home, my dearest girl. It is left to you in my will, my dear, and I have never told anyone that.'

'Oh—no——'

'Oh—yes! What did you think? That I would let it be sold when I go? Never. I know you will love it as I do. And don't worry, I have made ample provision for all my family—but you are special. You belong as no one else does.'

'I don't know what to say.' Was she dreaming? No. The pain was to real for any dream.

'Then say nothing. Just come as soon as you can.'

'I will. Uncle——' she hesitated. 'When we—Gregor and I—tell you what we have discovered, I think you'll be equally pleased.'

'Will I?' he smiled. 'If you say so, my dear. But I can wait. Rest now, and get your hand better.' He went back to his book, blew his nose with unaccustomed vigour, and wiped his cheeks. Victoria settled back with a little sigh, and closed her eyes. The decision had been made. And it was the right one, she knew. Of the one day in the distant future when it would be hers she thought not at all, but nevertheless, there was a warm glow, a sense of continuity, and that was important.

She must have dozed, for she heard quiet voices talking, and opened her eyes to see Gregor moving the table near the fire. He lifted it easily, set it in place, then looked across at her. 'Lunch is ready,' he said. 'Do you feel like eating?'

'Yes, I'm hungry.'

'Good. And there is fresh milk for our coffee afterwards.' He came over as she struggled one-handed to sit up, and leaned over, lifting her. She gritted her teeth.

'Thank you,' she said, but didn't look at him. Her skin no longer tingled at his touch, she resisted that. She didn't give a *damn* about him any more. The sooner he went, the better it would be. Until then, there were appearances to be kept up, for her uncle's sake, and only for him.

And then, after lunch they told him, and after all the upsets, it was still wonderful. Gregor's inexplicable mood had not managed to spoil it after all.

Uncle Craig sat, mouth getting progressively more open, as first Gregor, and then Victoria, and Gregor again, told of the gradual steps that had led to their discovery. The ancient photographs were produced, the written clues, and her uncle sat like a man in a dream, his delight so evident that once again, Victoria shared the surprise.

At the end, when all was done, Gregor went up for the dress from Victoria's room. She had hung it carefully in her wardrobe that very morning—

after—after—but she wasn't going to think about that any more, not ever again. Craig stood up to hold it. 'This would be a copy of Victoria's dress I should imagine,' he said. 'I can't see any material lasting so long—perhaps for Charlotte, who knows?' He stroked the fine silk gently. 'Ah, my dear, I would so like to see you in it—when your hand is better, of course.' He turned to Gregor. 'What news for your father, eh? Pity the phone's not working—we must keep trying them. There was a Telecom van not far down the main road when we flew here this morning——' even as he spoke, Gregor went over to the telephone in the corner and picked it up, listened, then shook his head.

'Never mind. Tomorrow, perhaps, tomorrow. Oh, this is all too much! What an exciting day I'm having!'

Victoria went over and hugged him one-handed. The pain in her other hand was constant, but bearable. 'We couldn't wait to tell you,' she whispered.

'And has she told you, Gregor,' Craig looked across at the large silent man standing by the fireplace watching them, 'that she is coming to live here?'

Victoria answered before he could. 'Yes, I told him.' It was, after all, he who made me see, she thought. Perhaps I have something to thank him for after all.

'It is good news,' said Gregor, who had not spoken for some time. 'Victoria told me of the parties there have been here in the past—she has told me a lot about Drummell House——'

'A party! Ah yes! I wonder if I can persuade

Robert and your mother to come up for Christmas—and Anne and Michael too.' He looked across at Gregor and said the words Victoria had been dreading since Gregor had spoken. 'Could *you* come here for Christmas, Gregor?'

Victoria straightened up slowly from her uncle's chair, looked across at Gregor, face still and silent. She could be poker-faced as him, she decided, if she chose. He wasn't the only one.

'I'm sure Gregor has commitments elsewhere,' she said. The unspoken words lay between them, and Gregor shook his head.

'Alas, yes,' he said. His eyes met Victoria's briefly, for just a moment, and both knew. No words were needed. 'It is impossible.'

'Well, never mind. You must be a busy man. And now, my children, if you'll excuse an old man who has had such a lot of news, I'd like a little rest.' He gave them an apologetic smile.

'Of course. Do you want to go to bed? I can fill a bottle——' Victoria began.

'No, no, I'll stay here, just close my eyes for a while.'

'I'll go and see if anything needs doing in the kitchen,' said Victoria. She didn't much care what Gregor did. She went quietly out, leaving the two men together.

There was not much she could do, single-handed as she was, but she wasn't going to sit there with *him*. She rinsed out a dishcloth, poured liquid cleaner on it, and began wiping down the kitchen surfaces. With the oven on, the room was warm. She had filled the kettle and put it to heat. It really was quite amazing, she decided, how you can

adapt to any situation. And she wasn't thinking
only of her head.

She had made herself a cup of coffee, found a
book, and was sitting reading it at the table when
Gregor walked in—but not from the hall passage,
from the back. He wore a parka and wellingtons.
She glanced up, but said nothing. He carried a
stack of logs, and damp glistened on his hair. 'Will
you open the door for me please,' he said. 'I wish
to take these to the hall.'

She got up, still without a word, and he went
out. She closed the door after him and sat down
again. She was not aware of what she was reading.
Aware only of Gregor, his face, his eyes, his bleak
expression. The sooner he goes, the better, she
thought, I don't want him here. And she bit her
lip, and took a deep breath. She looked down
again at the book, and the print blurred, and she
blinked hard, several times.

There was a funny 'ting' from the phone,
repeated, and she went over and picked it up to hear
the familiar burr of the dialling tone. Never had a
sound been so welcome! She ran along the passages,
through the hall, down the corridor towards the
main drawing room—and then stopped. She could
hear the drone of male voices. Gregor and her uncle
were talking, and for a moment she felt a stupid
shyness, shook herself, how ridiculous! and searched
for the handle. But the door had not been closed
properly and she heard words that stopped her in her
tracks, made her hand pause. It was Gregor who was
saying them. '—have never felt like this in my life. It
is almost frightening.'

'I'm a lot older than you. My advice is—tell
her——'

The woman who waited in Paris! Victoria's heart bumped. No wonder he could not stay—she could not stand there any longer, listening to what was not intended for her. She saw an image of a beautiful, laughing woman waiting, waiting—arms wide—and pushed the door open. Two faces looked round—were those expressions guilty ones? Did they wonder if she had been listening to their men only conversation? She lifted her head high.

'I—I came in to tell you the phone is working again,' she said—and, coward-like, fled, ran back to the kitchen, closed the book and got her coat and wellingtons on. Even if she couldn't walk far, she was going out. The words echoed in her head, hollow sounds, a jumble—it is almost frightening— have never felt like this before in my life—my advice is—tell her—tell her—tell her—— As she went out of the back door, along the track to the circle they had made, she heard again those words that had come before—and now they made sense. The words, faintly heard, not fully registering then, that had been spoken as she had reached the door. In her uncle's voice: 'We could meet the flight—of course you *must* do it—it would be wonderful, for her too.' That had been in those seconds before she heard Gregor's words. Wonderful for her—his woman to come *here*, to stay *here* so that Uncle Craig could meet the one Gregor loved?

She turned and looked back at the house, that gracious home she so loved. She did not want Gregor's mistress here! How could he even think of it? She stumbled on through mushy, melting snow, blinded by tears, cold now, her hand burning hot. It had all gone terribly wrong. So wrong. And now they knew the telephones were working, how much sooner would it happen?

On and on, towards the trees, fighting for every step, exhausted. Time to turn back, she was tired. She heard Gregor's voice calling her name—distantly, and ignored it. Heard it again and turned round reluctantly. She didn't want to worry her uncle. Gregor was standing by the back door, and had seen her. He waved, beckoning, and Victoria began to struggle back towards him. I'm not coming because you call me, she thought, don't think I am.

Nearly there, and she saw his anger, heard it in his voice when he spoke. 'Why do you do something so stupid?' he blazed, his voice hard and harsh.

'I went for a walk,' she snapped. 'I don't have to ask your permission!'

She pushed past him and into the corridor when she stopped and turned. He had kissed her here, once. He would not do so again. 'Leave me alone—don't come near me. *Leave* me! When my uncle's about, I'll talk to you, but when he's not, I won't, do you understand?'

'I understand perfectly—now that you have your old *lover* back—of course!' His face was white, almost grey in that shadowy place.

'He's not my old lover—he never was—and I don't want him——'

'I saw your face when you received his letter,' he shot back. 'My God—you trembled.'

Did I, she thought? Perhaps I did. But you love someone, don't you—you told my uncle, and *she's* coming here. She lifted her chin. Then she laughed, deliberately mocking, wanting to hurt him, although God knows, he wouldn't care. 'Ah, you

saw, did you? All right—yes, I do still love him—
and yes, now he's free, things will be different—
and yes—he was my lover. And a better one than
you!' And with that last, devastating statement, she
walked on, almost ran, into the kitchen, took off her
mac. He came in as she bent to take off her
wellingtons, and she looked up. 'Satisfied?' she said.

He looked at her, then walked away. She
watched him go, heart stricken with anguish. Why
had she said those things? She hadn't meant them.
She hoped she would never see anyone look like he
had looked then. It was as if he had been struck
very hard. Trembling, she bent and pulled off her
wellingtons. She wondered what would be the end
of it all. She could not bear this for much longer.
She felt sick, almost ill—and she felt utterly
wretched. With an effort she filled the kettle and
put it on the gas. Every move hurt, her head was
heavy, her hand throbbed painfully, her limbs felt
weak. She wondered if she had 'flu. Uncle Craig
walked in at that moment and she turned to him,
burst out crying and went to hug him.

'What is it, child?' he asked, perturbed.

'Oh, I feel—I don't feel well,' she said. 'I'm so
sorry—I——'

'Oh, darling, don't. Don't cry. It's delayed
shock from your hand, that's all. Why don't you
go up to bed, eh? Take a nice hot bottle——'

'I was going to fill one. You don't mind?'

'Mind? Of course not! We'll look after you.
What on earth did you go out in the snow for?
That was a bit foolish, wasn't it?'

She sniffed, managed a little smile. 'I just had to
get out. I'm sorry.'

'Here, sit down, let me fill that bottle and we'll

get you off to bed. Go on now, sit down.' He
pushed her gently into a chair, found a hot water
bottle and filled it. Suddenly, quietly, he said:
'Have you and Gregor quarrelled?'

She caught her breath. 'Has he said so?'

Her uncle gave her a wry grin. 'No. But his face
was like stone when he came in and told me he'd
called you back. He saw you from the window you
know, said something very picturesque in Russian,
and dashed out. Now, what is going on with you
two, would you mind telling your old uncle?'

She gave a huge sigh. 'I wouldn't know where to
begin,' she said truthfully. Craig gave her an
extremely shrewd look.

'You haven't by any remote chance fallen for
him, have you?'

Alarmed, she looked up—and he saw. He knew.
He smiled gently. 'Well, well,' he said.

'Please—promise me—you won't say a word.'

Uncle Craig handed her the bottle. 'Has it
occurred to you what's the matter with *him*?'

'I *know* what's the matter with him. I overheard
a bit of your conversation——'

'*Did* you now?' Craig raised a gentle eyebrow.
'And what did you hear, my dear?'

There came a low throbbing engine noise from
outside and she looked at her uncle in surprise.
'The old tractor,' he said, smiling. 'Gregor is going
to try and clear a path to the gate.'

'I'd forgotten about that! Good grief!'

'Yes, well never mind that. We won't be
interrupted—at least we'll hear him returning.
Now. What did you hear?'

'I didn't listen deliberately,' she hastened to
reassure him, 'honestly.'

'I know that. You don't need to tell me.'

'I heard——' she repeated as best she could the words she had overheard, and Craig listened, nodding, beginning to smile.

'Ah. I see. Yes. And what did you think it meant?'

'He has a woman friend in Paris—he—he's just discovered that he loves her, and she's coming over here and I don't want her to. Oh, uncle, I'm sorry, I know it's your house—but I—I couldn't bear it.'

He sat down beside her and patted her hand. 'You heard wrongly. It is not she who will be coming—but his father.'

'Oh. But he does love her—I——'

'Oh yes, he has fallen in love with a woman,' her uncle said gently—I'm afraid you're quite right there. And he will be seeing her and no doubt telling her——'

She shivered. That at least she had guessed right. 'Would you mind very much?' Craig asked.

She looked at him. 'I'll learn to live with it, eventually.' She was calmer now. At last she knew. The worst had happened. From there it could only get better.

'I'm sure you will,' he responded gently. 'You are a lovely girl, Victoria. The letter from Peter now, er, how is he?'

'Getting a divorce. He wants to see me.'

'And do you want to see *him*?'

She shuddered. 'No. When I came here, I thought I still loved him. For a moment, when I met Gregor, I thought it was him—just the faint resemblance, in the dark—I told Gregor just now—just before he came in to you—that I still loved Peter—I—I suppose I wanted to hurt him—although why he would care——' she stopped, her voice dangerously shaky. 'I'm sorry. Oh God, Uncle Craig, I feel so wretched.' He put his arm round her.

'Go and sleep now, you'll feel better. Here, take two more aspirin. I'll come up and see you in a little while. I love you, my darling, remember that.'

She swallowed the aspirins he handed to her, pulled a face, and said: 'And I love you too. Please—if you phone mum and dad, tell them I'm fine, and I'll phone later tonight.'

'Will do.' He nodded. His face was very kind. He was smiling, oh so gently. 'Off you go.' She didn't quite understand that smile.

She tucked herself up in bed, cuddled the bottle—oh, it was lovely and hot—and fell almost immediately into a deep sleep of utter exhaustion. And from somewhere far in the distance came the deep rumble of the tractor as it cleared a path through the snow-covered drive.

CHAPTER ELEVEN

VICTORIA awoke, and it was dark, and for a moment she did not know where she was. Then she remembered, as she heard the faintest of taps on the door, and called: 'Come in.' She had no idea how long she had been asleep.

She could not see for a moment who it was behind the lamp—then saw Gregor. He came in very quietly and put the lamp down on the floor, and sat on her bed.

'Where's my uncle?' she said, her voice like stone.

'Downstairs.'

'Then go and tell him I will come down. Please leave my bedroom, Gregor. We have nothing to say to each other.'

'We have a great deal to say to each other,' he answered.

'If you're staying, I'm leaving.' She pulled the covers to one side, was about to get out, when he put his hands on her arms and said:

'No. You will listen. And when I have finished speaking, then you may leave.' His grip was firm. How—*why* had Uncle Craig let *him* come up after all she had told him?

'Do you remember me saying that I had been searching for someone all my life? That I had never loved any woman, Victoria?'

'I remember. And now you've found her. Well, bully for you. Is that it? Can I go now?'

'It is you I love. Have loved from the moment I walked in and saw you.' She stopped struggling to be free, looked at him, thought—how cruel, how very cruel—and saw his face. Saw his face, and what was in his eyes, and went very still. The pain in those eyes could not be imagined, nor the drawn lines at his mouth. She opened her mouth to speak, couldn't manage, eventually whispered:

'I—don't—I don't——'

'Your uncle told me when I returned. Listen to me please, Victoria—this is not easy for me. I thought—Peter—you still loved him—when the letter arrived and I saw how you looked at it—my heart stopped. I knew then what I had been feeling all along was true. I was stricken with the most agonising jealousy, so unbearable I could hardly think straight. We were talking, your uncle and I, when you overheard part of what we said. Do you remember my words? I was telling him how I felt about you, because I knew I could trust him—and because I knew, from something he said that he had already guessed, and I said to him—and I think this must be the part you heard: "I have never felt like this in my life. It is almost frightening"—and he said: "My advice is—tell her." Is that what you heard?'

She nodded. 'Yes.'

'And it was of you that I spoke. Not my "French woman"—the one I said was waiting. I told you that to make *you* jealous—Yvette is an old friend, no more. Once, we were lovers, several years ago, but no more. What we have now is a friendship, that is all.' He took a deep breath. 'I had been haunted all my life by a picture I saw as a child. The picture of the first Victoria. And I think I knew even then, that one day I would meet you. I did not know how, or why, or when it would happen, but it was as if you existed for me all those years ago. Something began the moment we met—and perhaps fate decreed that it should be here we met, for this was the place, all those many years ago that your namesake met my great-great grandparent. Something began in that moment, some link was forged. Do you think it will be so easily broken. Do you not *know*?' His voice was scarcely more than a whisper, but she heard, and raised her hand, to touch his face. His cheek was damp. And then, at last, she knew the truth, and it was as if a great light shone into her heart. Her voice broke.

'Oh Gregor——' he kissed her hand, held it to his mouth, reached out to touch her with the other.

'Say that you love me, Victoria.'

'I love you. I have—oh—yes, from that moment too. I think I have always known it too.' He leaned forward and took her in his arms, and kissed her deeply. Huskily, he said:

'Do you remember me saying also that I felt as if I were coming home when I came here?'

'Yes. Oh, yes!'

'When we are married—could we live here, with your uncle, do you think?'

She had always known that, too. Had always known, somewhere deep inside her. And it was right. For he belonged here in a way as much as she did. 'Is that what you want?' She knew the answer anyway.

'Oh yes. I can open another ski and sports shop in Aviemore. I can commute—I can even teach you to ski, if you wish my darling.'

She began to laugh, clinging to him, laughing at the thought. 'Oh no, never.'

'We will see. Victoria—when you walked into the room last night——' Had it only been last night? '—in that dress, my heart stopped for an instant.'

'I know. You thought you'd seen a ghost.'

'More than that. I knew you would one day be my wife. My feelings this morning when I saw the letter from Peter were——'

'No. Ssh.' She put her finger to his lips. 'No. It's not important. He's no more important than Yvette. Less. He is nothing to me. Never was—and, Gregor—he was not my lover. I said that in temper—to hurt you.'

He gave a deep sigh. 'I know, I knew—last night—that you had never had a lover.' He closed his eyes. 'How soon can we be married? I want very much to make love to you again. But until we are married, I will not.'

'Before Christmas. Here in the church where I suspect our two ancestors—our namesakes—were wed.'

'Then that we shall be. Am I forgiven for my brutish behaviour?'

'Am I forgiven for mine?' she murmured.

He kissed her, and that was his answer. Then slowly, she got out of bed, and went again into his arms, and they clung to each other wordlessly, in silent communion, their bodies on fire with their deep endless love for each other, no more words needed.

And a month later, when they walked along the aisle in the tiny church, as man and wife, his father and mother were also there. The reception afterwards turned into a party that went on for two days and nights, but Victoria and Gregor missed it. They were skiing in the French Alps, well, during the mornings at least. . . .

Best Seller Romances

Romances you have loved

Each month, Mills & Boon publish four Best Seller Romances. These are the love stories that have proved particularly popular with our readers – they really are 'back by popular demand'. All give you the chance to meet fascinating people. Many are set in exotic faraway places.

If you missed them first time around, or if you'd like them as presents for your friends, look out for Mills & Boon Best Sellers as they are published. And be sure of the very best stories in the world of romance.

On sale where you buy paperbacks. If you have any difficulty obtaining them write to: Mills & Boon Reader Service, P.O. Box 236, Thornton Rd, Croydon, Surrey CR9 3RU, England. Readers in South Africa – please write to Mills & Boon Reader Service of Southern Africa, Private Bag X3010, Randburg 2125, S. Africa.

Mills & Boon
the rose of romance

Take 4
Exciting Books
Absolutely
FREE

Love, romance, intrigue... all are captured for you by
Mills & Boon's top-selling authors. By becoming a
regular reader of Mills & Boon's Romances you can
enjoy 6 superb new titles every month plus a whole
range of special benefits: your very own personal
membership card, a free monthly newsletter packed
with recipes, competitions, exclusive book offers and
a monthly guide to the stars, plus extra bargain offers
and big cash savings.

AND an Introductory FREE GIFT for YOU.
Turn over the page for details.

As a special introduction we will send you four exciting Mills & Boon Romances Free and without obligation when you complete and return this coupon.

At the same time we will reserve a subscription to Mills & Boon Reader Service for you. Every month, you will receive 6 of the very latest novels by leading Romantic Fiction authors, delivered direct to your door. You don't pay extra for delivery — postage and packing is always completely Free. There is no obligation or commitment — you can cancel your subscription at any time.

You have nothing to lose and a whole world of romance to gain.

Just fill in and post the coupon today to **MILLS & BOON READER SERVICE, FREEPOST, P.O. BOX 236, CROYDON, SURREY CR9 9EL.**

Please Note:- **READERS IN SOUTH AFRICA write to Mills & Boon, Postbag X3010, Randburg 2125, S. Africa.**

- -

FREE BOOKS CERTIFICATE

To: Mills & Boon Reader Service, FREEPOST, P.O. Box 236, Croydon, Surrey CR9 9EL.

Please send me, free and without obligation, four Mills & Boon Romances, and reserve a Reader Service Subscription for me. If I decide to subscribe I shall, from the beginning of the month following my free parcel of books, receive six new books each month for £6.60, post and packing free. If I decide not to subscribe, I shall write to you within 10 days. The free books are mine to keep in any case. I understand that I may cancel my subscription at any time simply by writing to you. I am over 18 years of age.

Please write in BLOCK CAPITALS.

Signature _____

Name _____

Address _____

_____Post code _____

SEND NO MONEY — TAKE NO RISKS.

Please don't forget to include your Postcode.

Remember, postcodes speed delivery. Offer applies in UK only and is not valid to present subscribers. Mills & Boon reserve the right to exercise discretion in granting membership. If price changes are necessary you will be notified.

6R   *Offer expires December 31st 1984*

EP86